A KISS TO TELL

WILLOW WINTERS

INTRODUCTION

A Kiss to Tell

I didn't need anyone to tell me; I knew he was forbidden with a single glance.

He was a boy I should've been afraid of, and definitely a boy I should've never wanted. No matter how much neither of those statements were true.

From the first time I saw him, Sebastian had a hard stare that pinned me in place. And years later, it hasn't softened.

We lived on the same street and went to the same school, although he was a year ahead.

Even so close, he was untouchable.

He was bad news and I was the sad girl who didn't belong.

One night changed everything.

We both had secrets. We both saw the pain in each other's eyes.

The gaze that gave me chills turned to a lust-filled haze that heated every inch of me.

But that didn't change who he was. A man who would take everything from me.

PROLOGUE

Chloe

THE KISS WAS BRUISING, just like his presence always was.

On the last Tuesday before school let out for the summer, and my ninth-grade year was over forever, Sebastian Black kissed me. No. He devoured me.

He destroyed everything I had in that moment. He took every bit and he made it his. *I* was his for that all-consuming kiss. My first kiss.

I still remember it so well. I couldn't breathe. I couldn't do anything but let the heat and electricity rip through my body as Sebastian pinned me against the wall. The rough brick scraped harshly against the small of my back, but I hadn't even noticed. I wouldn't notice until hours later, standing under the stream of water in a scalding shower. The sting I felt proved his kiss had left more than one mark on me.

His tongue was hot, his grip intense and his presence dominating as ever. When he followed me outside as I tried to hide around the corner behind the school, I didn't even see him coming. The chill in the air struck against my heated face as soon as the door swung open, and I could barely manage to feel anything but the cold sensation that flowed over my skin. I needed to hide. From the other kids, from the teachers who didn't care… from reality. I was always good at that.

I didn't expect anyone to follow me. No one had for the past few days. Each day proved harder than the last, although the nights were the worst.

I was still carelessly wiping away my tears—they were an unwanted nuisance just like how everyone else saw me—when I heard his hard steps behind me.

The sudden spike of fear I felt, paled in comparison to the effect Sebastian had on me. The sound of my startled gasp was dwarfed by the feel of my heart racing rapidly against his as he pinned me where he wanted me.

He always took what he wanted.

But I'd never once thought he wanted me.

His warm breath flowed over my face, and suddenly the iciness in the air was nonexistent. Nothing existed but him. Not even the air that separated us.

If I hadn't been stunned, the confusion would have shown on my face. I'd always wondered what it would be like to be kissed by a boy like Sebastian. I'd assumed it would always be nothing more than a passing thought. But every time he walked by me, every time I caught him staring at me, I knew there was something between us. His piercing gaze seemed to capture me in place while also looking right through me.

I was no one, but I wanted it that way. Not being noticed was the best thing that could happen when you lived where I did. Unless you were Sebastian, and then everyone noticed you and everyone feared you just the same.

He pulled away from me before I could react to his lips on mine, both of us gasping for air.

I'll never forget that his eyes were closed, or how slowly he opened them to paralyze me with those steely blues of his. A mask of indifference slipped over his face, but I know my expression showed my awe, my shock… my lust that I had so painfully hidden since the first day I'd laid eyes on him.

"Stop crying," he said, and his command was harsh as if my tears were an insult to him. As if my pain had anything at all to do with him. His nostrils flared and the rage he was so well known for was evident on his handsome features.

But just as it had never affected me before, it didn't affect me then either. I knew he was forbidden. I knew I was supposed to be afraid of him. Maybe I was just stupid because I never felt anything but desire for him.

"Stop fucking crying," he gritted out between his clenched teeth, "and don't tell anyone I did this. Not a single fucking person," he threatened. He brought his lips even closer to mine in a gesture that should have been menacing, but I'd be damned if it didn't make me hot for him where I'd never felt heat before. His eyes searched mine.

"Or else I'll make you cry those tears harder than you can imagine." His words caused my gaze to move from his lips to his cold stare. He would never know how hard I had cried in the middle of the night. He didn't know what had really happened and how guilty I was.

I shook my head gently and replied, "You can't."

His grin was accompanied by a huff of masculine laughter like he thought it was a challenge, but before he could say whatever was on the tip of his tongue, I cut him off.

"You won't make me cry. I know you won't," I said and shook my head, meeting his gaze with every ounce of sincerity I could muster. "And I won't tell anyone."

The last bit broke my heart in two, but I don't know why when there wasn't a single soul to tell anyway. There was no one I wanted to run to. No one but the boy who had lost control, kissed me, and obviously regretted it.

I watched as he swallowed, his throat tightening. The bit of stubble that ran up his neck tempted me to touch it. Whatever it was that had caused him to kiss me, whether it was only to silence my crying or something else, was gone. And I knew he'd never kiss me again.

Letting out a long breath, my lips still parted, I said nothing and let him walk away.

The masculine scent of a boy I should have feared and a boy I should have never wanted, was all that filled my lungs as I tried to steady myself. I sagged against the brick building and tried to make sense of what had just happened.

I stopped crying that day and didn't shed another tear. Not that week, and not at the funeral. Not when my uncle let me move in with him, so I would have a place to stay.

I never spoke of what happened and I started to question my sanity when he never spoke of it either.

Nothing changed in the way he acted, or in the way he looked through me.

But I remember the way I touched my lips as he stalked away.

I remember how it felt and how it was everything I needed in that moment.

HE COULD NEVER HAVE KNOWN what he'd done to me that day.

But neither of us would ever forget.

CHLOE

Five years after the kiss

RANDOM STREETLIGHTS GOING out is something that used to terrify me.

I hate the feeling that comes with the sudden flicker signifying what's about to happen. Then the light burns out, and all you're left with is darkness. Even just remembering how it's happened before makes me shudder.

One night two years ago, it took place in quick succession, the bright lights flickering briefly and then suddenly there was no light at all. It happened on my way home from old man Bailey's hardware store. I'd gone only an hour before sunset and spent longer than

I thought I would. Some asshole had kicked in my front door the night before and there was no way I was going to leave the store without a new lock. I bought two just to be on the safe side.

And so, I was walking home alone in the dark when the lights went out, one after the other. I couldn't walk fast enough to get to the next light that hadn't burned out; I nearly ran to it.

I don't like to be outside at night, not unless I'm on my porch. But even then, I'd rather stay inside, where the idea of safety used to mean something.

Either way, I'd spent too long at the store and with the plastic bag dangling from my wrist, I quickened my pace when the first bulb died. I remember how I stared straight ahead at the next one, praying it would give me light long enough to get home. As if it was listening to my fears and wanted to mock me, the light vanished before my eyes.

Fear of darkness is reasonable. But the kind of inevitable dread that lingers when a light goes out while you're watching it used to follow me everywhere.

It haunted me during the day and never hesitated to steal my sleep at night.

I don't know when things changed, but as I make my way down Peck Avenue, the light flickers on my right and I don't miss a step, I don't even dare to look at it. In my periphery, I see shadow consume everything behind me. My fingers wrap a little tighter around the strap of my purse, but it's more instinctive than a conscious response.

My heart races and then steadies to the sound of my heels clicking rhythmically on the pavement.

One more block and I'll be home. In darkness or in light, it doesn't matter anymore. I've been through both.

I keep my eyes fixed straight ahead and think about the mundane task awaiting me at work tomorrow. I spent all day organizing Mr. Brown's new clients, and my back is killing me from leaning down to the filing cabinet and then looking at the computer, time and time again. A few more days and the new system will be in place. At least until he decides to change it again.

I used to think Marc Brown changed the system so frequently out of boredom, but after looking at his client list, I think the lawyer is a crook. Everyone in this city is, so it shouldn't have surprised me. I'd work for anyone else, doing anything else, but my options aren't exactly overflowing.

I have my high school diploma, but after trying for the last two years since graduation to get into any college at all and being rejected, a diploma is all I have and all I'll ever have. And that piece of paper is useless here.

My phone pings in my purse and I'm more than eager to pull it out.

I could use something to keep my mind from

wandering back to the shit job I have. As I pull out my phone I see the old book I'd stowed in my purse earlier this week, ready to read the novel again. For the dozenth time.

A court-mandated shrink gave it to me five years ago. She loved to draw, although I remember thinking she wasn't really good at it. I used to have a picture from her of a duck she drew with a pencil. I don't know where it's gone, not that it matters much. I still have the books she gave me and, more importantly, a love of books. I wasn't so much into the drawing, but that shrink—I think her name was Rebecca—gave me a handful of fiction. She gave me a way to get lost in someone else's world. It wasn't long before I started writing as well, trying to create an escape from this life. I couldn't give two shits about her artwork, but I'll always be grateful to her for giving me a love of reading and writing.

Forgetting about the book and everything that happened back then, I focus on the text message.

You'll never guess what happened last night.

It's Angie, a friend from work. Well, I think she's my friend. She's new and doesn't do much but read magazines and chew gum while she tells off clients who want their paperwork faster than she can print it out, but she tells me all the details of her Tinder dates. I'm the only one she talks to at the office.

Mr. Brown exclusively hires girls in their twenties

—and younger. Of the five of us, Angie likes to only talk to me. I get it, sort of. I don't care for the other women either. For the most part, they ignore me, which I'm used to, but they also stop their hushed whispers the moment I walk into the room. At first, I thought it was all in my head, but no, they like to talk about me. About the rumors of what happened years ago. *How sad it is.* They can go fuck themselves.

My family has history here, but it's no secret. Every person in this damn city comes from circumstances of shame. Luckily, I don't work with them much; it's usually Angie who I get paired with, and I should really be grateful to Marc for that.

What? I text her back, curious about the escapade of last night.

After dinner, I took him home and he was fucking amazing in bed. I think I'd use the word... enthusiastic.

My brow raises at the last word.

What does that mean? I ask her.

He did things to me I had no idea I even wanted.

I can feel my blood heat just thinking about what she may have done. I've never done anything with anyone. Having sex simply isn't on my to-do list. I'm not interested, not from anyone in this city. My phone pings again, and I look to see what else she's said.

He choked me.

I stop in my tracks for a moment, staring down at

the glowing screen in my hand and rereading what she wrote.

And he told me he was going to take my ass and holy shit Chlo, anal is e v e r y t h i n g.

If anyone could see my face, they'd see the shock. I don't know how she can even surprise me anymore. My fingers reach up to my throat as I swallow, wondering why he'd want to do that to her and how she could enjoy it. The choking part. I watch my fair share of porn, but that's one I don't really understand.

I'll tell you more on Monday, but I had to tell SOMEONE. I read her text as if she'd spoken it to me, sprightly voice, and all.

Can't wait to hear all the deets. My reply can't convey my gratitude at being informed via text about the choking, so I can hide my naivety and shock from her at the realization she's into that.

You almost home? she asks, and a soft smile plays at my lips. A warmth I'm not used to courses through me and slowly I find my pace again.

One block to go, I answer her and wait for her to respond with the same thing she wrote a few nights ago. For me to tell her when I get in.

Last week I told her I live just outside of Fallbrook, and she kept pushing to know where exactly. When I told her I'm from Crescent Hills, the same city as Mr. Brown's office, her face paled. She's not from around here, but she knows the reputation of this place and what it's known for. Everyone does. If you want a taste of sin, Crescent Hills is where you'll find more than your fill.

I'm used to the embarrassment, but not from someone who chooses to work in this city. She doesn't have to be here any longer than a nine-to-five, and honestly, I don't know why she even chose to work in this run-down area when she lives in the big city. And that's exactly what I challenged her with when she told me I shouldn't be walking home.

I'm grown. I'm aware. I'm also broke and on my own since my uncle died two years ago, leaving me with bills, a mortgage, and no job to pay for any of it, so I told her she could take her high horse and shove it. But maybe not in those exact words, and maybe with a choked voice of shame.

The silence lasted only a minute or so, but it felt like an hour. She offered to walk me home and when I declined, as politely as I could, she snatched my phone from my desk. Before I could ask her what she was doing, she texted herself before handing it back, so we would have each other's number.

Text me when you're home, she told me, but I didn't answer her. When she texted again, apologizing, and asking if I'd made it home all right, I answered only because I thought she was genuinely worried. And things have been normal again ever since.

It's a small act of kindness, but it means more to me

than it should. I'm smart enough to know that I shouldn't let it get to me like this. I can't rely on anyone or trust anyone. Outsiders come and go here. Even Ang said she wasn't planning on staying at the law firm for long. I should know better than to think of her as a friend.

But when she sends texts like the one that just came through, I can't help but feel a little camaraderie. I smile as I reread the text. *See you Monday, prepare to be scandalized!*

My heels click on the asphalt, worn rough from years with no repairs. In the distance, I hear a siren, and farther down the block, a few kids are screaming at one another. It's nearly ten at night, but this is normal.

Just like the streetlights going out.

Back when I would have childish fears about the darkness swallowing me up, I also used to dream. I used to dream of leaving here. Of going anywhere but here and never returning. I wish I could forget those memories. But they cling to me like the filth that clings to the gutters on the side of the road.

I used to dream of running away. Mundane things like bills have a way of robbing you of your fantasies. At least I have my books and my writing. Even if I never escape this place, I can still escape into the worlds I build for myself in my stories.

Years ago, when I was still in school, I told my uncle

that I'd leave here one day. I remember the sound of the porch swing as it swayed, how my fingers felt as they traced the rusted chain that held it in place. He told me this city didn't let anyone leave. It kept them rooted to this place.

I didn't know what he meant until he passed and there was no one here to pick up the pieces. No one but me.

My feet stumble and I come to a halt as I try desperately not to fall forward. The combination of rubble on the ground and the sight of someone's shadow laying across the very porch swing I'd just been thinking about are what almost cause me to trip.

My chest aches with a sudden pounding of anxiety. No one comes to visit me. It's one of the blessings I've been afforded by being the sad girl with her sob story. I keep my head down and I mind my own business. No one likes me, no one but Ang, and no one fucks with me either. Why would they? I have nothing.

But someone's there. I can't see their face, but the shadow is there and unmistakable.

The paint on the porch swing is weathered, and no one ever sits on it anymore, but I watch the empty seat move back and forth and then a man steps away from the shadows.

A man I see from time to time, but always in passing. Except for when I think of him late at night. Unfortunately, it happens more than I'll ever admit.

He's a man I used to want because he made me feel something I'd never felt before. A mixture of hope and desire. Like the silly dreams of getting away from this place, I used to want to be his. To be pinned down by his hands while his eyes held me in place.

I used to dream of him pressing his lips to mine and stealing my breath with a demanding kiss. I knew he could do it; I'd felt it once before.

His stubble-lined jaw looks sharper in the night with only the neighbor's porch light and the pale moonlight casting shadows down his face. My heart beats slower, yet faster all at once. Knowing Sebastian is on my porch waiting for me, I can hardly breathe, let alone move.

His steely blue eyes are next to come into view, and they immediately capture me. Staring straight at me, they pierce through me and see more of me than anyone else can. He must. I can feel it deep in the pit of my gut. He's always been able to do it. There was never a moment where Sebastian didn't have that power over me.

With clammy palms, I try to move my hands, but my fingers are as paralyzed as my body. It's not from fear, although I know that's what this man should elicit from me. That's the reaction he has on everyone else.

No, it's not fear. As a gust of wind blows, I sway gently in the breeze and it seems to free me from the spell his sharp blue eyes have placed on me. I refuse to look back into his gaze.

Instead, I stare at the chips in the old cement stairs that lead to my porch and feel my heart squeeze harder and tighter than it has in a very long time.

"What do you want?" I ask Sebastian in a hoarse voice, barely louder than a murmur.

His shadow shifts in my periphery, but I don't look up at him.

He's a man I would let do whatever he wanted to me. I would let him do completely as he pleased. There's no reasonable explanation for it. No justification. I'm fully aware that he'd chew me up and spit me out.

Maybe everyone has a person like that. That one person you know can destroy you, and you pine for it despite yourself. I crave what he's capable of. I want the bad things that come with the promise of being his. That confession alone is enough proof I belong in this shit city.

I can feel the danger, the dominance, the overwhelming presence that never leaves with Sebastian Black. I can even smell his masculine woodsy scent that sometimes filters into my dreams. With my lungs full of it, I close my eyes, letting it intoxicate me, but doing my best not to show it. I won't give him that satisfaction. Not when he chooses to give me nothing. Not when he pretends that I'm nothing to him. Although maybe I am. Why would I ever be more than nothing to a man like him?

"Why are you here?" I ask, hardening my voice, raising it, and daring to finally look at him. His shoulders fill the entrance to my front door. My *open* front door. It creaks and the sound echoes in the chilly night air as Sebastian looks me up and down, the hint of a smirk on his face until his gaze reaches mine again.

"I thought you were smarter than that, Chloe," he says and his deep voice rumbles. It's rough, and the way he says my name sounds dirty, even though he's only said it in the same manner as always. With a wanton heat building in my core and my breathing picking up, I stare into his eyes as he adds, "I'm here for a little chat... with you."

SEBASTIAN

*C*hloe looks so damn tired. It's obvious that her hair must have been up all day; I can still see the impression of where a band was wrapped around her wavy brunette locks. She swallows thickly, and I swear I can hear the faint sound even from where I am feet away from her. Even with the clamoring from the Higgins kids yelling down the block. With a heavy breath she looks up at me, and I can see she's biting her tongue in reaction to me telling her I came to chat. She's done it for years. The questions shine in her doe eyes though. They stare back at me with the well of emotion that runs deep between us.

The bags under her pale blue eyes only make her look that much more beautiful. I don't know how that's possible.

Every time she comes to mind, I tell myself I'm picturing her differently than she is. That whatever it is that attracts me to her, plays tricks on my memory and makes me think she's more gorgeous than she really is.

And every time I'm proven wrong when I see her.

"You going to let me in?" I ask her with a smirk on my lips. One that makes her eyes narrow.

"Seeing as how my door's already open," she starts off strong but has to take a heavy breath before she finishes, "why don't you be my guest?" She gestures and the purse on her shoulder slips down her arm. Although she struggles to grab on to it, she doesn't take her eyes off mine.

The tension between us is thick, but it's always been that way. From the second I saw her in tenth grade, until this very moment, there's something about her that draws me in like a moth to a flame. I know I get to her too, but only one of us can be the fire.

"After you." I push open her door a little wider and wait for her to pass me. She takes the stairs slowly and then quickly walks by me as if she's trying to get away from me as fast as she can. It's not the first time she's done that and the reaction it sparks in me is the same.

The desire to chase her.

The first time it happened, it didn't come over me until the school year was almost over, and I knew I wouldn't get my weekly dose of fantasizing about Chloe Rose from across the lunchroom anymore.

I gave in and went after her, and it only made the sweet, sad girl who stared back at me that much more desirable.

Kicking her front door shut and locking it, I keep my back to her until the light flicks on. I can hear her drop her purse and then continue walking to the back of the hall. She leaves me at the front door in silence, so I have to turn around and face her.

Her house is just like the rest in this area. All the townhouses here are original and were built by the same company that ran the steel mill. They were made for the workers employed by the mill.

Until it shut down, just like the coal mines did, leaving everyone in houses they couldn't afford, with jobs they didn't have anymore.

The slate floors have gouges in the corner; my guess is something heavy hit them, and then I remember what happened two years before. The tension I'm feeling evaporates and anger comes flooding back at the reminder. I take a quick look over my shoulder toward the door, but even through the somewhat recent coat of paint, I can see where the wood broke when it was kicked in. The main lock's been replaced, and there's an additional one above it.

I wonder if she thinks of that night every time she locks the door. I thought about telling her who did it. Marley was an addict who picked houses at random for items to fence to support his habit. Stealing anything and everything he could was his method. He got his last hit the night he stole from Chloe, leaving fear behind that didn't stray from her eyes for months.

He got his high and then fell to the bottom of the river where I dumped him.

Everyone in this city knows I have my limits. They didn't know Chloe was one of them until that night. I stayed away to keep the target off her back, but people don't forget in this city.

I may be young, and I may work for a man who doesn't venture into this territory, but I run these streets where she lives. No one owns Crescent Hills. If I wanted to take it though, there's not a single prick here who'd stand in my way.

But I don't want this city any more than it wanted me.

I want Chloe Rose. The thought catches me off guard. I've always known it's true, but I don't like to admit it. There's something about her that begs me to be something more for her.

That's the part that kills me though; there's nothing more to me than what she sees, what everyone sees. A ruthless man who's angry at life and makes his living by beating the piss out of pricks.

She's not like me. She's soft and kind and needs a gentler hand than I can give her. She deserves better.

"How'd you get in?" Chloe's voice is soft, although

the edge of defiance is still there. Bringing my gaze back to her, I take her in again. From her long legs and skinny waist to those wide hips that beg me to bend her over and give her a punishing fuck, the sight of her makes even the misery of why I'm here vanish for a moment.

She crosses her arms as if she doesn't agree with what I'm thinking, but all that does is put a strain on the blouse she's wearing and push those gorgeous tits of hers together. They may be small, but all I need is a mouthful. My dick stirs, and I have to look away, heading to the living room and glancing around at her place as I go.

"I picked the lock," I tell her, although it's not true. I have a set of keys, got them the day she ordered them from the hardware store. It kept her waiting longer than she should've been there, but I had to do what I had to do. And that meant sneaking in later that night to make sure she was sleeping. Which she never did, but Chloe has a habit of missing sleep.

As do I.

So, she laid there quietly in bed and stiffened at the sound of me moving about, but she never turned around, she never dared to check. She has a habit of that too. Of thinking if she ignores the monsters she conjures in her head, they'll go away. The sad fact is sometimes those monsters in the dark aren't imaginary, but damn does she like to convince herself they are.

She huffs out a laugh that's flat and then brushes her hair back as she leans against the side table in the hall. "You making yourself at home?" she asks, daring me to keep walking and make my way to the living room. I don't answer her, still taking everything in and noting that it's all the same.

She hasn't changed a thing. Not one thing in this place for two years. For some fucked up reason, it sends a ripple of pain through my chest, more than the broken door did. The walls of the hallway still have the same framed photos her uncle had put up after she moved in with him.

Her uncle was more of a parent to her than her own mother was. Him taking her in after her mother's death was the best thing for her, but he was supposed to help her get out of this shit life, not have a heart attack and leave her here all alone.

"Come on over here and have a seat with me," I tell her as I sink into the large sofa that takes up half the room. The edges of the armrest are worn, but it smells like her. Exactly how I remember Chlo. A soft peach scent and some kind of flower. Nothing but sweet.

My fingers dig into the cushion as she stalks slowly to the opposite side of the sofa and seems to consider sitting down as she stands in place. She smooths out the back of her skirt as she stares at the seat and then kicks off her heels, letting the silence pass.

All I can do is stare at her, even as she refuses to look back at me. It makes me think about different possibilities. If we lived in a different city. If our lives were different. If any of that were the case, I never would have let her think she was anything but mine. There's something in my soul that recognizes her as belonging to me. She's mine to protect, to take in my bed, to give the world.

Brushing the rough pad of my thumb along my lip, I have to remind myself that's not the world we live in and she's not mine. Life is better for both of us that way.

I'm a threat to those who have control of the neighboring territories. And that little fact never leaves me. Especially after what happened last week.

I'm no good for Chloe.

She needs someone to take her away from here, and away from me.

Finally, she sinks back into the sofa, sighing and taking a peek at me. "Just tell me what you want, Sebastian."

Those eyes transfix me. It's like she sees through the bullshit, but she always has.

What I *want*. That word sends a wave of warmth and desire through my body. I want her. But that's not what I'm here for and she's something I'll never have.

"Have you been watching the news?" I lean forward as I ask her the question, resting my elbows on my knees. Her small body stiffens as she shakes her head. As if watching the news is a sin.

She's a horrible liar. The worst liar I've ever fucking met. Maybe that's why I feel so drawn to her. She can't hide from me. But I can't hide from her either. There's something so freeing about that simple fact. Something that makes being in her presence addictive.

Even if it's for a shit reason.

"Barry turned up yesterday, did you hear about that?" I ask her and immediately feel the waves of anxiety rolling off of her. Anything that triggers memories of her past causes her pain which is easily seen by anyone who would bother to look.

"I don't give two shits about Barry." Her voice turns harder as she pulls her knees into her chest. She stares straight ahead, and I follow her gaze to the peeling wallpaper.

"Do you know who did it?" At the question, her head whips in my direction with a bolt of anger flashing in her eyes.

"I don't know shit," she bites out and her defensive-ness is exactly what the police will latch on to. "I'm going through a lot right now," she adds, but her voice wavers. Her gaze falls as she visibly swallows and tucks a lock of hair behind her ear before peeking back up to the wallpaper. "I don't want to think about any of it."

Her voice lowers to a murmur as she says, "Sure as shit, not Barry."

As time slowly passes, her anger diminishes, and I watch as she returns to her typical quiet state. She's nestled in the sofa with the sad smile she always carries gracing her lips. Picking at the hem of her skirt, she glances at me thoughtfully. "Is that really what you wanted to know?"

"How are the nightmares?" I ask her, feeling my chest get tight as the smile vanishes and her eyes shift to a hollow expression I hate and know all too well. She's good at hiding. Hiding her pain behind a smile. Hiding her reality behind the thought that one day she'll get out of here. Well, she used to, anyway. She used to be good at all of that.

Time changes a lot of things.

She starts to answer me, but she can't hide the emotion in her voice. Before she can lie and tell me she's fine, her voice hitches and she turns her gaze toward the empty hallway.

"Why do you care?" Her words cut deep. Chloe's pain is clear, but does she really think I don't care about her?

She's smarter than this. It's the second time tonight I've had that thought. "You know I care," is all I give her. But for the first time since I stepped foot on her porch, I feel the mask slip from me, letting her see what's inside without putting up a wall for her to break through.

She can see it all anyway. If I stop trying to hide, maybe she will too.

She still hasn't answered my question though.

"So how are you handling them? The nightmares?"

"They're back. I've had them every night since Saturday," she tells me. Saturday. The day they caught her mother's killer. She's back to fidgeting with the hem of her skirt as her gaze flickers between me and the floor.

"How did you know?" she asks, peeking up at me and I almost allow myself to get lost in the pain reflected in her baby blues. I'd rather be lost in hers than mine.

"You look tired," I answer her honestly. She drops her gaze though, sighing deeply and pressing the palms of her hands against her eyes.

"Well if you wanted to know if I knew who killed Barry, I don't. So, you can go now, and I can get some sleep." She stands up and hugs her chest, although her posture is more aggressive than defensive.

For nearly a year, I could feel her watching me whenever I was near her. The pull to be at her side was stronger than anything else. Nothing could compete with her, but I resisted. I couldn't let her get caught up in this shit.

Now she's the one pushing me away. Fair enough, I

suppose. It doesn't change the fact that this is a small world, and I know she still feels that draw, just like I do.

"I have something that can help you," I tell her as I stand with no intention of walking out just yet. She can pretend that she has the ability to tell me what to do. We both know that's not the case, but I respect her too much to rub it in her face. Besides, I can't let her push me away when I have something she needs.

"What is it?" She's wary but curious. That's the Chloe I know.

Reaching into my pocket, I pull out the vial I prepared before coming here and roll it between my fingers. "It's something to make you sleep."

"Drugs?" she scoffs and shakes her head at me, letting out a sarcastic laugh like I've gone mad.

"It's something you could get at any pharmacy," I offer her, letting a smile slip onto my lips.

That's not completely true. A friend gave it to me to see if there'd be any interest for it on the streets, but people in this city want harder drugs. Drugs to help them forget, to escape, even if just for a short time. I thought it could help Chloe though.

She's a good girl, but she needs this. The sweets will knock her out and give her the rest she so desperately needs. I would know.

"You're a bad liar," she says, and the irony doesn't escape me.

"I'll put a few drops in your tea," I tell her as I walk past her, brushing my arm against hers and feeling that familiar combination of heat and want seep into my blood. Her quick intake of air is all I need to keep moving forward, walking to her kitchen before I hear her take even a single step.

I go right to where I know she keeps her mugs and tea as I hear her walking toward the kitchen.

"I don't drink tea at night," she tells me, and I know she's lying again. Glancing at the box in my hands, I show her the label then pull out what I know is her favorite mug. She picked it up at a used bookstore last year. If she's not working or home, she's always at that bookstore.

"Decaffeinated tea then?" She only crosses her arms aggressively again and leans against the small table in the kitchen. "I'm getting tired of you lying to me tonight," I add with my back to her as I fill the mug with water and put it into the microwave.

When I turn to her, the hum of the microwave filling the room along with the tension between us, she meets my gaze with a hardened expression.

"How many years will go by this time? You know, before you barge into my life, then pretend I don't exist the next day?" She sounds bitter, but I know it's fake.

I cluck my tongue, keeping my eyes on her face instead of her chest. But with her arms crossed like that, she's not helping me. "Would you really want me to make this a habit?" I ask her, not realizing how much I actually care what her answer is until silence is all I'm given.

I already know the answer; I shouldn't have asked the question.

"What do you want from me, Sebastian? It wasn't to ask if I'd heard about some asshole getting mugged."

"It was." I wouldn't have come to see her if I didn't think I really had to be here. I don't like what she does to me. How she takes over every sense of reason and consumes my thoughts long after we've parted ways.

"The cops are going to question you about his death. I need you to tell them you don't want to talk about it. Because otherwise, you'll look guilty." The microwave goes off and I go back to making her tea when she starts to answer me.

"I didn't do it. I--"

"I know you didn't. But you look like you're lying when anyone brings up anything that has to do with your mother. Which is why it could be pinned on you."

With the bag of tea steeping, I stiffen at my own words. A sick feeling stirs in the pit of my stomach. I know what it's like when someone brings up shit you don't want to hear. How all of a sudden, you feel a coldness and pain all over like it's taken over everything inside of you.

I reach for the sugar on the counter and stir some into her tea. She doesn't object or ask how I knew she would want it. The spoon clinks gently against the ceramic and Chloe still hasn't responded, but when I turn to her, her eyes are glossy with unshed tears. I feel like a prick.

"This doesn't have anything to do with that," she says, although she barely gets out the words.

"That's not what the police think. Two bodies were found right after they caught the guy who killed your mom. You don't need to watch the news to know what the cops are thinking."

She starts to object, but I stop her and say, "Just tell me you won't talk to them." Grabbing the vial, I put three drops in her tea, making sure she's watching me, then set it next to the sugar.

"What could I possibly tell them?" Her tone is as tired as she looks, and she doesn't hide the pain that lingers beneath her words. "I don't know anything."

"They're looking for someone to blame. I don't want you to give them a reason to think that someone could be you." I know they tossed her name around as a possible suspect. She has motive, and emotions are raw for her. They want the case closed, and she's an easy target.

My throat feels tight although the words come out steady as I tell her, "If they come around, I need you to tell them you don't know anything, and you don't want to talk to them. That's it."

I hand her the mug I've prepared for her, my palm

hot as I rotate it so she can grab it by the handle. "It doesn't matter how they'll push you for more or what they say. They want you to talk, and you're not going to. All you're going to tell them is that you don't know anything, and you don't have anything to say, right?" I ask her, and she nods obediently and with an understanding that supplants the sadness. The cops here are crooked and covering for whoever lines their pockets. Anyone can take the fall, and they'd be perfectly all right with that.

She takes the mug with both hands, letting her fingers brush against mine. The small bit of contact sends electric waves up my arms and shoulders, igniting every nerve ending and putting me on edge. So much so, that my body begs me to either step away or grab her wrist. But I do what I've always done. I resist. I let myself feel the discomfort of not having her but being so close that I could easily have her if I just gave in.

She's closer now, taking a half step toward me, her head at my chest and her gaze on the floor as she blows across the top of the hot cup of tea.

"I understand," she tells me, her lips close to the edge of the mug, but she doesn't drink it yet.

I reach over, one hand on either side of her head, and brush back her hair. She stares up at me with a longing I remember so well. A longing I've dreamed of for so many nights. The air is pulled from my lungs as I

33

stare into her eyes. "Drink your tea and go to bed, Chloe." My words are rough, and it's hard to swallow. The moment her baby blues close with her nod, I get the fuck out of there before I do anything stupid. Anything that would put her in even more danger.

CHLOE

I'll never forget her screams.

The second I hear the front door open as Sebastian leaves, it's all I can think about.

As I set down my tea on the kitchen table, not even Sebastian's lingering heat and scent can provide an adequate distraction. No, the moment he brought up my mother, I knew the memories would come back and they wouldn't leave.

Sebastian never stays for long. Never. No matter how much I wish he would.

Closing my eyes and gripping the edge of the chair, I take in a deep breath. I know I need to lock the door, but I'm desperately trying to calm and steady myself.

At war with the memories of that night my mother died are the thoughts of Sebastian having been in my house just now.

He was here for business. But whatever the reason, he doesn't want me to say anything, and so I won't. I don't have anything to say to the cops regardless, but I am emotional, and I could see myself spewing all sorts of hate for the dead man whose murder could easily be pinned on me.

Whatever Sebastian is involved with, and whatever his intention is behind telling me to keep my mouth shut, I'm grateful for it.

This addition to my tea, however, I don't know what to think about that. I don't know what it is, and I don't believe him when he said it's something I could get at the drugstore. I may be attracted to him for some unknown reason, but I'm not fucking stupid. The thought resonates with me as I turn the locks on the front door.

It was the nightmares that led him to me the first time. Or my reaction to the nightmares really. The constant crying.

It was five years ago when I was in ninth grade and he was in tenth. I turn around as a chill flows up my arm, traveling to the back of my neck and causing every hair in its path to stand on end. I'd sag against the hard door if my body wasn't frozen at the memories.

Her scream. *Screams.* The shrill sound still wakes me up at night, tears streaming down my face as I try to keep my heart from leaping out of my chest.

When it happened, I was cross-legged on the floor

of our townhouse one block down from where I am now, and my friend Andrea was on the sofa.

Justice Street. Ironic isn't the right word for the name of the street I grew up on. It's pathetic and riddled with agony that the word is allowed to exist in this city. I know now that she was nearly two blocks away, in the alley right across from both the park and the bars she had frequented.

The fact her screams carried that far, is evidence enough of how desperate she was for someone to help her.

The first scream came at 11:14 p.m. I remember how the red lines of the digital display shone brightly on the microwave's clock.

"What the fuck are you doing?" Andrea asked me with wide, disbelieving eyes as she slapped the phone from my hand. It fucking hurt. The memory brings the sting back, making my left hand move on top of my right. Absently I rub soothing circles over it, staring straight ahead although I don't see the hall to my uncle's home. Technically, it's mine now, but I don't want to feel any sense of ownership for a damn thing in this city.

She coughed on the hit she took from her blunt and I remember the sound so clearly.

All I see is Andrea's angry expression, but fear was also evident as she locked her eyes with mine. My heart beat faster back then, knowing I needed to call someone to help whoever it was that was screaming. But now it beats slow at the memory as if my body wishes I could stop time. As if it's doing everything it can to try to make that happen, to go back.

I heard another faint cry for help and Andrea followed my gaze to the open window. The smoke billowed toward it. I sat there numbly as she quickly ran to the window and closed it.

"We have to call--" I tried to plead with her, knowing deep in the marrow of my bones that whoever was screaming was in agonizing pain.

"No, we don't," Andrea pushed back, waving the smoke from her face. "The cops can't come here," she argued with me. "Someone else will call... if whoever that was even needs help," she told me, but both of our eyes strayed back to the window at the muffled sound of another shrill scream.

I didn't move to my phone.

Instead, I took a shower. Of all the things I could have done, I stepped into a stream of hot water, listening to the white noise of the shower, praying for the water to wash the feelings away. The guilt, the disgust, all of it.

But that's not something water can do.

When I stepped out of the shower, I swear I heard it again, but it sounded exactly the same. Andrea said I was crazy and that it was all in my head. That it was only the one time anyone had screamed at all, which she corrected to two when I stared back at her.

The last faint cry I heard was well after midnight. Andrea convinced me it was just a couple fighting; the Ruhills were good for that on the weekends as they were both angry drunks who spent their paychecks at the bar, but now I know that's not true.

Over an hour had passed. And no one went to help her. Not me, not a single person in this city.

It was nearly 9 a.m. when the police banged on the door and I answered. I thought my mother had lost her keys and locked herself out. It wouldn't have been the first time. When I opened the door, it still hadn't dawned on me that the screams had belonged to her.

She was the one I didn't help save.

No one did.

Not a single person for blocks around helped her.

Andrea wasn't the only one to close the window and tell the cops that's all they'd done. Screams in this place are a constant. Cries for help come often. And everyone assumed someone else would call the cops or offer street justice. But it didn't happen that way.

That fucker, Barry, the one who turned up dead in the news today, I'll never forget how he laughed at the bar as he bragged to anyone who would listen about how he'd turned up his television because she wouldn't stop screaming. He'd shut the window and turned up the volume until he couldn't hear her cries anymore.

He'd heard her, he'd known she was begging for help, and yet he did nothing and dared to be arrogant about it.

It was easier to hate him than it was to hate myself for knowing I could have helped her. I could have tried to help her. I could have done something, anything—rather than listen to Andrea.

I never spoke to her again. Not that she cared much. With my mother gone, there'd be no one to fill my medicine cabinet with what Andrea referred to as the good shit.

The terrors that came with my mother's death are justified. I deserve so much worse. I would do anything to go back. *Anything*.

My numb body finally moves to prevent what's coming next. The memories of who my mother truly was, an abusive alcoholic who never wanted me. They're joined by the fears I had back when I was a kid, that she was coming to punish me. That I deserved so badly to be punished.

"She's long gone," I whisper as two kids yelling up the street remind me that I'm here, in my uncle's house, only a block away from my childhood home. And even farther away from where my mother was raped and murdered. More importantly, it's years later.

As my tired eyes yearn for sleep, I walk slowly down the hall back to the kitchen. The chill of the memories follows me. It took all this time to find her killer, a fifty-year-old man who'd once been a high school teacher. They found him dead in his house three cities over. They only know it was him because he was being prosecuted for the rape of some other young woman and the DNA matched. He killed himself rather than being taken in last Saturday.

That wasn't even a week ago, and then Amber Talbott died a few days later. She saw and heard everything, yet she did nothing but record part of the attack and send it to her friend. It wasn't enough to solve my mother's murder.

Shot from behind, it only captured the back of the man who'd done it as he viciously punched my mother, shoving her deeper into the alley. Amber had claimed she sent it to her friend because she was scared, but the texts between them implied otherwise. I know the video; I can see it clearly now. It's only half a minute long and was taken from Amber's window across the street.

My mother saw her in those final moments, or at the very least she saw the phone. Up until the moment I saw the video, I thought the worst thing you could see before being murdered would have to be your killer's eyes. But that's wrong. It has to be. Because how horrible would it be if the last thing you ever saw was someone hearing your cries, knowing you were in pain, but choosing to do nothing? Or simply walking away, shutting their window, or worse, filming it for their own amusement.

Amber said she thought the guy had just mugged my mother and then moved along. She told me to my face that she was sorry, and she wished she could have done something else. I didn't believe her.

She could have done something if she'd really wanted to. She was older than me. She was closer, too. She could have sent that video to the cops. Five years later, just days ago, someone mugged her and left her for dead in an alley next to the hair salon where she worked.

No one did anything to help her, either.

And now Barry's dead. Two people who I hated so much for so long, both killed within days of each other and after my mother's killer was found dead.

Barry was an old man who couldn't be bothered unless you wanted to talk about the winning lottery numbers or placing bets. Horses and the tracks were his favorite. I used to like him because he'd show me pictures of the races. But when I heard how cavalier he was when it came to my mother's murder, I couldn't stand the sound of his name, let alone the sight of his face.

I'm glad he's dead. And if I'm being honest, I'm glad Amber's dead too, but it doesn't change the root of my pain.

Nothing can change the past. Nothing can take away the guilt.

I feel empty and hollowed out as I walk back to the kitchen table. The chills refuse to leave me.

Just as the nightmares don't. But I had those even before my mother died. They were my constant companion, just like the bruises back then.

The night terrors got worse after she was gone, but the bruises eventually faded.

Staring at the cup of tea, I reflect on Sebastian. I remember how being around him, being *kissed* by him, took so much of the pain away. Even just thinking about him helped.

But I'll never be okay. It's only a pipe dream. Sebastian may pull me away, pull me closer to him and into his world, but it's only temporary. He's proven that too many times for me to put much faith in him at all.

I grab the cup and dump it in the sink, watching as the dark liquid swirls down the drain.

I don't want to sleep. My mother waits for me there.

SEBASTIAN

I can still feel her fingers against mine. Her touch hasn't left me since last night. My mind wanders to what she would have said if I'd told her I wanted to stay.

The rumble from the engine turns to white noise as I think about all the ways I could take the pain away from her. I imagine lying in bed beside her and taking her how I've dreamed of for as long as I can remember. My grip tightens on the steering wheel and the breeze from the rolled-down window pauses as I slow to a stop at a red light.

The radio station being changed to something else grabs my attention and I have to clear my throat and adjust in my seat to play off what was going through my mind. Carter changes the station again, but he's not going to find what he needs by picking a different song. There's nothing in this world that's going to help take his mind off of the pain.

"You staying with me tonight?" I ask him. His dad kicked him out of the house again. Not that the kid did a damn thing wrong. He's sixteen and involved with the wrong crowd, namely me, but he never does anything wrong. Not since his mom got sick last year.

He flicks the radio off, choosing silence over the commercial on the last station.

"I don't know," he tells me solemnly and then falls back against the passenger seat, staring listlessly out the window. Chewing on his thumbnail, he avoids looking back at me.

Which is fine, because the fucker behind us yells at me to get going while honking his horn. The red light's turned green. One look in the rearview, catching the driver's gaze silences him. He sees who I am, and suddenly the pissed off expression on his face vanishes. I wait for a beat, then another as the assholes settles into his seat and averts his eyes, waiting for me to do whatever the fuck I want to do.

I'm careful as I step on the gas, and more careful with what I say next. "How's your mom doing?"

Even that simple question gets him worked up. Carter shakes his head but doesn't say anything. He tries but he's too choked up.

Carter's mom keeps asking for him to help instead of his dad. It ranges from changing her position in bed

45

and helping her go to the bathroom, to just being by her side to talk. His father doesn't like that though. He's a drunk and a deadbeat.

With five boys and her health deteriorating, I can only guess his mother is hoping that Carter will take care of the others when she's gone. He's the oldest. Hell knows his father won't.

"Let's talk about something else," he suggests as I turn down Peck Avenue. "Like where we're going?"

My lips kick up in a half smile at his response. He texted me earlier, asking me to pick him up, but didn't question where I was taking him. He asks so often now, almost every day. I guess he doesn't care where we go so long as he has somewhere to get away. He always goes home though. For his mother. For his brothers too.

"I want to check on someone," I tell him as I round the corner, passing over a speed bump and slowing down at the weathered stop sign that marks that we're close to our destination.

Carter's brow furrows. I don't know if I've ever told him I want to check on someone before, but when I turn down Dixon Street and slow in front of Chloe's house, he gives me a shit-eating grin. As if I just told him his favorite joke.

"Like old times," he says with a rough laugh. Carter's my only friend and that's because I know who he is to his core. He's six years younger than me, but he's like family, the only family I have.

All he has are his brothers; he's told me that so many times. But it's always followed up with a pat on my back as he tells me I'm one of them. I have to admit, it's nice to feel wanted, and even nicer to feel like you're part of a family. Even if you know deep down that's not really true.

I was eighteen and he was twelve when we met. He got caught shoplifting bread of all things. Dumb fuck couldn't even pick something that fit under his jacket.

Grabbing him by his collar, I yanked him away from the clerk hellbent on beating the shit out of him. If you let one person get away with stealing your shit, everyone will come running with duffle bags.

So you have to send a message, loud and clear. I was in charge of keeping that shop out of harm's way; it was one of my first jobs from Romano.

I looked the clerk in the eye and told him the kid was going to pay for what he'd done. I had a reputation and the clerk was happy enough to let me handle it, knowing he could tell his story about how I'd kicked the kid's ass for trying to steal from his store.

Carter was a scrawny thing and still is, although he's starting to fill out. I picked him up like he was nothing and he didn't try to fight it.

The look of fear in his eyes wasn't there, only a look of disappointment, even as I dragged him around back.

I remember how I felt something I hadn't in so long. Something like regret, maybe?

He wasn't like the others, the ones looking for a fight.

Carter already had enough to fight for and to fight against, so to him I was just one more thing he had to endure. I could see the weary resignation in his eyes.

I didn't kick his ass. Instead, I told him to go home. I made the decision to let him go because he wasn't like the others. And also, because the idea of beating up on a lanky twelve-year-old made me sick to my stomach.

That was when I saw his anger and his fight. His passion.

"I'm not going home without it," he told me with determination, even though his voice shook. His hands balled into fists, but he didn't raise them.

"Get home, kid," I told him, walking over to where I'd thrown him and towering over him.

He stared me in the eyes as he shook his head. "I'm not leaving without it."

"For a fucking loaf of bread, you're willing to get your ass beat?" The kid was stupid. I still tell him he's stupid and it's true half the time.

"I have to make sandwiches, my mom told me--" He started to say something else, but I cut him off.

"Well your mom can make it herself," I spat back at him, with a pent-up rage he didn't deserve. He was only a kid, and some of the kids didn't know. My mother was a whore. A bitch. I don't have a single nice thing to say about her. Even with her dead in the ground after spending the last minutes of her life with her favorite needle, I can't bring myself to say one good thing about her. I never had a family aside from my grandmother, bless her soul. And I never would. It's as simple as that. It was as deeply ingrained in me as whatever possessed Carter that night.

"She can't!" he yelled at me. I took one step closer to him, and he stiffened. My spine was stiff, my shoulders straight and the aggression and threats evident just from my stare at him.

His bottom lip quivered as he took in a quick breath, but he didn't give up. "I have to feed them tonight and we don't have anything... but I can make sandwiches." He gritted out the last words with tears in his eyes. "I just need bread."

"And what are you going to put on the bread? You going to steal something else too?" I berated him, even though I believed him.

"There's peanut butter already."

"You can eat it with a spoon," I said dismissively, turning my back to him and ready to get the hell away from him. Something about the way he looked and acted bothered me to my core. He wasn't frightened, and he wasn't angry. *He was desperate.*

"She said to make sandwiches for my brothers-"

I lost it again with the kid, thinking about my own

mother and how she'd forced me to fend for myself. She never told me to make dinner, I just had to. No one else would. "And why didn't she do it then? Huh? She can dish out orders, but-"

"She's in the hospital. She told me on the phone to make sandwiches and I just need bread." He stumbled over his words, but he never took his eyes from me. "I told him, the clerk," he gestured to the shop, "we'd pay him, but I don't have the money right now." He visibly swallowed and continued, "My mom will pay him when she's back. And it's going to be real soon. She'll be okay real soon." He started rambling on and on and I could feel his sob story getting to me. I could feel myself getting played like I'd played everyone else as I grew up on the streets.

"So, you're stealing bread to make sandwiches for your brothers?" I lowered my head to his. "Here's a hint, kid. When you're told to do something, you don't have to follow it to a T." I licked my lower lip, slipping my hands into my pockets and expecting him to give up and go home already. To leave the corner store alone and my reputation intact and go eat the fucking peanut butter out of the jar like a normal asshole would.

But he didn't get what I was saying.

"Are you dumb?" I asked him as he stood up, faced me and held his ground.

"She said to make them sandwiches. I'm not leaving until I get the bread."

I searched his eyes for the longest time before going in and grabbing the bread for him. But I followed him home, telling him I wasn't going to give it to him until I saw that he was telling the truth. I knew he was one of the kids who lived on the edge of the city. I remembered seeing a bunch of them out that way. I make it a habit to know everyone and for them to know me.

If he was lying to me, he'd learn real quick to never do it again.

I didn't know that he had four brothers, or that their place was a mess because they'd just moved in. I heard they were on the run from where they came from, but I didn't know that their mother was in the hospital because of their grandfather. Apparently, he's who they were running from and he'd found out where they ran off to. Which is how his mom wound up in the ER and why their father in jail as a result of it all, paying Carter's grandfather back for what he'd done to his mother. Leaving five kids alone in a new place without a damn thing to eat.

I didn't know, and I didn't care, not until I saw how happy they were just to eat. Even something as simple as peanut butter sandwiches. I asked him how long it'd been since she went to the hospital.

It had been four days. And they were starving, but

he'd promised his mom he would feed them, and he did.

Twelve years old, and he was the oldest of five. She stayed in the hospital for another three days before the doctors would let her come home. Now she's back in the hospital, but not with bruises and broken ribs. Two years ago, she was diagnosed with cancer. She's been fighting it all this time, but Carter's still taking care of his brothers, and now her too.

That was the first time I met Carter, four years ago. I took him under my wing at first, but now he's a friend. A friend who's been through some shit and is still in it. He has a family though and a reason to fight. I've only ever fought to stay alive or to rule with fear. That difference is something I'm not sure he'll ever understand.

"Is she home?" he asks me, and it brings me back to the present. To being on the other side of the city, close to my place and in front of Chloe's.

Letting out a sigh and running a hand through my hair, I shrug like I don't know.

"You like her," he tells me like it's a fucking joke. He doesn't know what's going on. Not entirely, but even if he suspects it, he won't ask. He doesn't like to look for the darkness, not when he's surrounded by it already.

"She doesn't need me asking her out," I mutter under my breath and ignore Carter's eyes pinned on me.

It takes a second and then another for him to start putting the puzzle pieces together.

"You going to tell me why we're here?" he asks me with a brow cocked. He's feigning lightheartedness; concern is clearly etched on his face.

I've told him more than once that he doesn't pay attention enough. That life is shit, it always will be, and either you accept it for what it is and protect yourself, or you fall victim to whatever fate chooses to inflict on us. But given the weight of what I'm hiding, I don't tell him. I don't want it to be real.

I lie to him and say, "I just wanted to see if anyone was snooping around here."

"Cops? Or Romano's people?" Carter asks and the gravity of either of the two options sends a chill down my spine. I can handle the cops, Chloe can't. But neither of us could handle Romano if he decided to go after her. He runs the territory up north and I work for him on occasion. I may be his muscle, but I'm not sure even I know the extent of the shit Romano's involved with.

As I'm thinking about the last fucked up thing Romano had me do, Carter asks something I wish he hadn't, because it's too close to being true. "Is this about that thing Marcus gave you?" His voice is even, but his expression's fallen.

Pushing back in my seat and hiding my anxiety, I tell him, "I told you not to mention that."

He only nods and seems to shrug it off, like it doesn't matter if Marcus is the reason we're here. Both of us know that's bullshit though. Even saying his name is something no one likes to do around here. Romano may run the territory up north from us, he may even make an appearance down here on occasion when he needs something, but you always see him coming and he's only dangerous because of the men he controls.

Marcus is a different sort of threat. By the time you see him coming, you're already dead. He doesn't have a territory, he doesn't have men. When he makes demands, they're always about death. They called him the Grim Reaper when I was younger. He doesn't want money, he doesn't bargain. What Marcus decides is final and there's no room to negotiate. He's only one man, but he's killed every man who's crossed him and even more men simply because they were on his list.

A minute passes before Carter reaches for the radio again and lets the music ease the tension.

"It's fine." My words come out casually as I watch Chloe's house. Not a thing looks out of place. It's not fine though. This shit is exactly why I could never be with her. One day you're on top, the next you're in a ditch. That's how this lifestyle is, and I'll never bring anyone into this shit life if I can help it. That especially goes for Chloe Rose.

"When are you going to ask her out?" he asks with a wide smile. He still has happiness in his soul. Enough to bring a bit of light to every dark situation. One day it'll go out. It always does for men like us. But I'll do my damnedest to keep it from happening.

"I know you want her," he chides again.

He doesn't know the half of it. I've known Chloe for a long time. And I made sure she never knew how I watched over her when her mother died. She wasn't okay. Everyone knew it. Just like they knew I wasn't okay when my mother died.

No one gives a shit though. People die, and somehow you keep going.

Then more people die and one day it's you.

One time I walked up to her porch and peeked in her window after she'd moved into her uncle's. The TV was on and I thought maybe she was watching it. That she'd be okay. It had been weeks. Weeks of nothing but her crying, constantly crying and hating herself. And I despised it. I fucking loathed it. The whole street could hear her uncle yelling at her to stop crying. That he'd lost his sister too and that she needed to stop.

When I looked in, she was still crying, but her eyes were wide open, her cheeks tearstained, and she saw me.

I know she did, not that it changed anything. I knew at that moment when she didn't do anything or say anything, that I was just as dead to her as her mother was. It hurt me like nothing else in this world had to know that just then, I meant nothing to her. I couldn't take her pain away. I was nobody special.

I'd never been more sure of anything in my life. I was nothing that night.

But the next day, I proved her wrong. When she kissed me back, I proved her wrong.

CHLOE

*H*e comes by every day. Friday night he stood in my kitchen. Saturday, he drove by with Carter Cross, Sunday he came alone and now it's Monday night and he's outside again.

I act like I don't see him. I've always done that. Everyone leaves you alone if you act like you don't exist.

The thing about Sebastian though, is that he doesn't leave until he knows I know he's watching me. Or maybe that's just what I think because I feel his gaze on me every time and I have no desire not to look back at him.

I pull back my curtain when the car outside idles and idles. A book is open in my hand, its pages unread. I let it shut as I peek outside to see who it is. The large text closes with a dull thud that matches the single pound in my chest when I see him out there.

I try to swallow but my throat's dry.

Angie said it's an intimidation tactic. I shouldn't have told her anything about Sebastian coming by like this. She concocted about a dozen theories of what's going on with the murders and Sebastian and why he's checking on me and instructing me on what to tell the cops. She was animated, to say the least, but I was more interested in hearing about what she did on Sunday with her new boy toy than anything that has to do with this shit city.

My eyes drift down, meeting Sebastian's and instead of glancing away, I hold his gaze for a moment.

I would feel it, wouldn't I? If his intention was to intimidate me, I'd feel fear, or a chill maybe? I'd feel something other than the quiet stillness that settles deep in my bones, the smoldering heat that simmers in my blood. Just looking at him, my body relaxes.

I swear I even see his lips tug into an asymmetric smile when I don't look away.

My heart does that thud again, and I have to loosen my grip on the thin curtain and let my head fall back against the headboard.

He'll only ever be at arm's length, so this power he has over me, this innate emotion he controls inside of me, can't be good.

The idling stops, fading into the sounds of the night

and that warmth and soothing feeling disappear with it. It's sickening that something so small could garner so much emotion from me. As I reach for my book, I see my phone out of the corner of my eye.

I don't have a fucking clue where I left off. My fingers run along the edges of the pages as if my memory can lead me to the right page, but all I can focus on is the phone.

Shoving the book off my lap, I reach for it.

The cops didn't come to question me. I text the number I know is Sebastian's. He's never explicitly said it was him and usually he texts me, but I know it's his number. I want to tell him he can resume pretending I don't exist.

When he doesn't reply, I skim through the previous messages.

The first one reads: *You did good today.* He sent it a few nights after the infamous kiss. The night I first slept peacefully in this house after my uncle took me in.

Who is this? I asked, but he never answered.

When I first moved in, my uncle didn't have a spare room ready for me. We'd had to clear out the cluttered room he sometimes used as an office. Almost all of my mother's things had to be thrown away in the move. Same thing with some of my possessions, not that I had much. This townhouse was already full, and I wasn't even sure if I was staying here for long. No one told me anything. No one but Sebastian in a nameless text.

The phone pinging in my hand scares the shit out of me, spiking my adrenaline and forcing my heart to race up my throat. I nearly slam my head back against the headboard, but somehow manage to calm myself down.

The memories of the week my mother died have always haunted me. That week brought awful night-mares, ones that have come back in full force now that the past is being dredged up.

It's only Sebastian, I tell myself and breathe in deeply, calming every bit of me, although the task feels even more impossible than staying awake long enough to see what he's written.

How are you sleeping?

It's fitting he would ask that just as I rub my eyes with the palm of my hand and feel the sting of the burning need to sleep.

I chew on my lip, my fingers hovering over the screen. I don't want to lie to him here, not on the phone; I don't want to taint these messages that mean so much. After a moment I tell him the truth and see exactly what I expect in return.

Not well.

Have you been drinking your tea?

The vial is on my nightstand, staring at me as if I'm to blame for this shit. I nearly took it last night, but I don't do drugs. Not any sort. I've seen what addiction can do. Although I've also seen what desperation can do. And I'm desperate for one night where I close my eyes and I'm not haunted by memories of the past. I was doing so well for years. Her murderer being found is what set everything off. And the nightmares have come back with a vengeance.

Take it. His message sends a chill down my spine. It's as if he can hear my thoughts.

It takes me longer than I thought it would to write him back. Mostly because I don't know what his answer will be, but I know what I want to read.

If I take it, will you leave me alone? I text him and then grab the vial. I don't have a cup of tea handy, but I have a glass of water. Without even thinking, I put one drop, then another, then the third.

I watch the liquid swirl as I wait for his message. The other night I thought it was clear, since in the tea I couldn't see its color.

But it's pink, a pale, pale pink that quickly disappears in the water.

Before I take a sip, I check my phone only to see he hasn't responded. The lip of the glass feels cold as I bring it up and take the first gulp, wondering what it will taste like.

It tastes like nothing at all. Maybe a tinge of sugar. Just a faint hint.

I'm still considering the taste when the phone goes

off on my lap. *You need to sleep.* How typical of Sebastian to respond without answering my question.

He has no fucking idea how badly I need to sleep. I'm delirious.

I chug the rest of the glass and intend on telling him that I drank the stuff he gave me, or maybe telling him something just so he'll stay with me on the phone until I've fallen asleep.

That doesn't happen though. Instead, I stare at the empty glass, feeling lightheaded and drowsy all at once. My sense of time begins to warp, feeling like it passes slowly but quickly just the same.

I barely get the glass on the nightstand before the darkness takes over. I'm able to slip under the covers, feeling the weight of sleep pulling at me. And I give in to it, so easily.

* * *

"You're late." Tamra's voice is clear as can be. She always had a slight rasp in the last word of every sentence and she kept her lips in the shape of that word for what seemed like an odd amount of time.

Where am I? I can feel my brow pinch; this room is familiar, but not so much that I know where I am. The carpet's thin and worn out in front of the television where the car seats are. There are three of them, although they're empty now. No one's here but me, sitting on the sofa that's just as worn as the carpet and Tamra, who's standing in front of the open door.

"He made me stay overtime." My mother's voice drifts in through the tense air. She's agitated and suddenly anxiety runs through me.

"Well, then, this is overtime for me. I can't watch these brats for free."

I'm not a brat. I swear I was good. I was good. I want to tell my mother, but I know to be quiet. With my hands in my lap, I wait stiffly. I'll only move when I'm told, I'll only speak when I'm spoken to. With my throat tight and dry, I wring my fingers around one another and glance at my bookbag at the end of the sofa. It's already packed, and I didn't forget anything. I never forget. If I do, I don't tell my mom and I hope she doesn't find out.

"Of course, you're gonna fucking charge me," my mother spits out her anger at Tamra. Anger which I know will be directed at me on Monday when she watches me again unless she tells my mom she's not going to watch me anymore without being paid early. Which she's done before. In that case, I stay in my room all day and don't answer the door. But Mom got in trouble for doing that once.

"Let's go, Chloe." My mom barges into the living room as Tamra stays where she is, keeping the front door open. It's late and I still have homework to do, but I don't know how to do it. I don't know how to read the words and I need someone to tell me, but Tamra won't and Mom's mad so I know better than to bother her.

I can tell from the way she stomps across the room it would be a mistake for me to do anything or say anything. I get up quickly. But I have to be quicker. If I move fast enough it won't burn when she grabs my arm.

"I'm coming," I tell her as fast as I can, snatching my bookbag and scurrying to her side even though fear is racing through me and begging me to run.

I'll be quiet; I'll go to sleep. Miss Parker will help me. It's only second grade, she keeps telling me I have time to do it at school if I get there early, but that I have to learn to read. I'm trying. I promise her I am.

"You see how no one helped me?" I hear a voice from outside this moment, a voice that sounds so close, so real. So full of rage and vengeance. My mother. Fear runs down my skin and up the back of my neck, freezing me where I am as I swear I feel her hot breath at the shell of my ear.

She didn't say that in the memory. She's telling me now.

I look back at Miss Tamra, still trying to keep up with my mother, even though her grip tightens so hard it's going to bruise. My blood runs cold and a scream is caught in my throat at the sight of Tamra leaning against the back wall, her left hand on the sofa. Blood coats her hair where a bullet wound mars her skull and it leaks down to her cheek, dripping onto her collarbone. I blink and suddenly she's standing there, yelling at my mother that she's an ungrateful bitch.

The chill doesn't go away, the sight from just before still stealing my breath and sanity.

The hand around my arm twists, burning my skin where

my mother is touching me. It hurts. Mom, it hurts! I scream out, but the words don't come. I'm no longer there. It's dark and the bruising hold changes to something else, feeling like the kiss of a spider climbing up my arm in the darkness. I try to jump back, but I'm trapped, with nowhere to go and I can't see a damn thing.

She's here. My heart races and dread ignites inside of me, but I can't run. I can't see her. I can only hear her so close to me.

"No one ever helped me," she tells me. "They're going to pay for that."

* * *

It felt so real last night, the sensation of my mother being so close to me.

An uncontrollable shudder runs through me as I slowly walk down the stairs. My heart won't stop racing and I can't clear my throat. I feel like I'm suffocating.

It was only a dream.

It's only a dream.

My chest tightens and the fear rips through me anew as I swear I hear something upstairs, something in the bedroom.

"Knock it off," I grit between my teeth.

The floor behind me creaks, loud and heavy. It almost sounds like someone's walking down behind me quickly and not hiding their weight, making me scream and I nearly fall down the last four steps. My back pressed against the wall and my chest frantically rising and falling, I stare behind me. No one's there. No one's here.

"It's only a dream," I remind myself and ignore the flow of ice that rolls over my body and how every hair on my body stands on end as I remember my mother's words. *They're going to pay for that.*

I'm not crazy, but I feel like I am. Crossing my arms over my chest, I feel my blunt nails dig in and remind myself that I'm alive.

The night after my mom died, I had the same type of dreams. The ones where she felt so real, following me even when I woke up.

"Please, go away," I beg her as I fall to the floor, sitting on the steps and wishing the wave of coldness that keeps coming over me would go away. Go away forever.

I told you, I hear my mother's voice, but I know it's just a memory.

She's not real. This isn't real.

The dead don't stay away for long. And they'll pay. Every single one of them will pay.

SEBASTIAN

*I*t's been three years since Romano gave me this job. The knife slams down on the cutting board as the thought hits me. I grab the carved meat and put it in the tub with the rest of the chunks.

I'm the butcher of a shop that rides the line of his territory. When Romano hired me to work here at Paul's Butcher Shop, I thought it meant something different. I thought it meant he was hiring me to be a part of his crew.

Now I know better; he just wanted to watch me. Train me, or maybe mentor me if he ever needed someone like me. The line of customers coming in for their packages distracts me and I glance up for a moment. Eddie, Paul's son, rings them up one by one. I stay in the back with a few other guys, processing all the orders and occasionally we have to stay here later, after closing hours.

Like when Romano has a special order.

Picking up the butcher knife, I slam it down with my teeth gritting together. This isn't his turf, but I'm not ready to start a war or gather an army against him. There's no one here to recruit, just the addicts who camp out behind the line of the highway that separates his area from Crescent Hills.

Most of the meat here is shipped off to God knows where. This place sees plenty of money come in and go out, but the numbers don't actually add up. We're just doing his bidding.

Still, I cut the fucking carcass up like I'm told, and stay on the right side of a would-be enemy while I have to.

I vaguely wonder how long that'll be. And when the time comes, which side I'll be on.

The bells hanging over the front door bells, two cheap bells that ding and then ding again as the door is open and closed quickly.

My gaze rises and goes back down, only to rise again with an unsettled feeling flashing through me, to take another look.

Chloe's not dressed to be out in public. She's in pajama pants and a baggy t-shirt with sneakers that aren't even laced like she couldn't get out of the house fast enough. Her hair's down and windblown.

"What the fuck is she doing here?" I mutter beneath my breath and drop the knife on the cutting board. Before I can even wipe my hands off, she's brushing past Eddie, ignoring him completely. She doesn't hesitate to go around the counter and make her way back here. "Sebastian," she gasps my name with a mix of relief and desperation.

My heart pounds harder as every man and woman in this place watches us. I can feel all their eyes on me as I keep my shoulders straight and head to the sink to wash my hands. I'm trying not to let her or anyone else see what I'm feeling deep down in my gut. This isn't a good look.

"I need you," Chloe speaks before the swinging door that separates the kitchen from the front of this small shop even closes.

The adrenaline pumps harder in my veins.

"Aren't you supposed to be at work?" I ask her although my gaze is focused on Eddie. I try to swallow but can't, so instead, I watch the water run down the drain before turning off the faucet and drying off my hands. She doesn't answer me, but she steps closer to me at the sink.

"What are you doing here?" I ask her in a harsh tone with no room for her to question how I feel about this shit. No one comes here. No one who knows any better. *She* should know better.

Her baby blues flash with something—shock, or

anger—I'm not sure which. Her loose t-shirt nearly slips down her shoulder as she takes a step back. The place is silent save the exhaust fans as she takes a moment to look me up and down.

"I need you," she tells me honestly, with a sincerity that everyone could hear, even if only spoken in a whisper. She brushes her wavy hair behind her ear and moves her gaze to the vinyl floor of the kitchen, blinking away the emotions ravaging her. The muscles of her throat tighten as she wraps her arms around herself. "Do you have a minute?" she asks as if she didn't just run back here and disrupt everything while having no consideration for what she's doing. The type of danger she's putting herself into.

With a deep crease in the center of her forehead and a pained expression in her eyes, she tells me again, "I need you." It's the third time she's said it since she got here, but she's never said those words to me until today. Fuck, I can't describe what it does to me. Her left foot kicks the floor as she slowly seems to notice everyone else as if they didn't even exist before.

I watch her gaze as it moves to Eddie, who's looking at me curiously and I give him an icy stare until he looks away.

I know he tells Romano everything that happens and having her come in making a scene like this is something that would get his attention. Talking to me about something as if I can save her... that would get his attention too. Romano needs to know everything, or so he tells us. But I don't plan on telling him shit.

Especially because it's her. And the way she's going about this is going to cause problems.

That anxiety comes rushing back, not just from what everyone else is wondering, but also from what Chloe has to say.

"Aren't you supposed to be at work?" I ask her again and toss the hand towel onto the steel counter.

"Angie keeps asking me that too," she mutters beneath her breath. Swallowing thickly, she looks over her shoulder before gripping my forearm and whispering, "I need to talk to you."

Her pale blue eyes plead with me, sinking deep inside of me like she always does. And for the first time in so long, I wish she wouldn't.

"Did something happen?" I ask her innocently, every hair on the back of my neck standing on end. I can hear people moving again, going back to their business, but they're quiet and slow to move. They're listening to everything.

"Did you see the news?" she asks me, and I stare back at her straight-faced as I shake my head no. I already know what's coming before she keeps going. It's only now that I regret going to see her; I invited her to think she could rely on me. She doesn't know what she's doing though, and all the shit I'm in right now.

"Tamra Stetson is dead," she tells me in the barest of

whispers as if she's speaking a sin in the holiest of churches.

She has no idea what she's doing. She doesn't know how everyone is watching her. Watching *us*.

This city will talk, and word spreads like wildfire. That could be dangerous, but I already knew I was fucked. I just can't risk her going down for this.

"Why don't we go out back?" The question is really a demand as I grab her elbow. Her gasp is short-lived as she walks quickly beside me and my grip on her tightens. Using my forearm, I shove open the back door and pull her out back. The heat and the sun are blinding for a split second.

There may be no one out here, but there are plenty of people watching. Listening. It'd be naive of me to think that Eddie is the only person keeping tabs on me for Romano. Waiting to hear something they can use against anyone who has anything they could want.

Like her.

Chloe hisses between her teeth as the door closes with a loud clack. "Did you have to be such a dick?" she asks me with a fierceness I fucking love.

She rips her arm away and the action makes her shirt slip off her shoulder, showing me more of her soft skin and the dip in her collar.

The second she sees me looking there, she pulls it back into place.

"You should know better than to come here," I warn

her, keeping my voice low, making sure she hears the threat. She's reckless, beautifully so, but it's dangerous. Right now, I can't have it.

"I need you, and--"

"It can wait," I cut her off, feeling my heart slam harder. Every time she says those words it does something to me. It rips me apart knowing how badly I want those words to be true and how wrong she is.

"But Tamra--"

"No one gives a fuck about Tamra." My answer is brutal, and I bite it out quickly, defensively even. Enough that I notice the change in my tone, but she doesn't.

"You don't understand, I wrote this list." She barely gets the words out before shoving half a sheet of paper against my chest. It's ragged like it was ripped from a spiral notebook and crumpled up before being smoothed out. It looks old as fuck and takes me a moment to recognize what it is.

Seeing the column of names on that piece of paper sends ice through my blood.

"Each in order," she says, and I hear her swallow before she looks back up at me. "It's every name in order."

Amber
Barry

Tamra

Mr. Adler

Dave

Andrea

"I DIDN'T PUT last names, but look at them, look at the list." She doesn't have to explain it for me to know. "It's happening right in order," she continues and struggles to breathe as if every word is suffocating her.

All the recent deaths have taken place according to this list. First Amber, then Barry, and now Tamra. Everyone knows about Jeff Adler. He'd been with Chloe's mother that night in the bar bathroom. He told the cops he'd heard her screaming but didn't feel like dealing with her. He's a piece of shit, always has been.

"Why would you even write this?" I can feel my anger and the tension in my body. The heat that's running in my blood, but the sight of her changes it as her hands wrap around my hand holding the note.

"Tell me it's a coincidence," she begs me with a choked voice. The tears in her eyes linger and she only stares at the paper, rather than returning my gaze that I know she can feel. She struggles to breathe again and then covers her mouth.

When she lifts her eyes to mine, everything in her begs me to answer her with what she wants to hear.

"Tell me this is all a coincidence, please. I keep dreaming about them. My mother and..." She trails off, but her regret and remorse are palpable. She shakes her head when I don't answer, as I stand there stunned by the raw emotion and innocence.

"I'm just going crazy, aren't I?" she asks me, and I let the tension between us wane. I give her a moment to calm down as she lets out a hard breath of air. "I'm just having these nightmares and--"

"Was there another name?" I ask her, cutting her off, and rub my thumb against where I can feel the indentations from a pencil. Where it's obvious she put her own name down before erasing it. I know it was there, just beneath Andrea. I know it.

She chooses to go the route she always does with me, she lies, shaking her head and sending her hair swishing around her shoulders.

She grabs the piece of paper, trying to calm herself down and collect her composure.

"I wrote down the names of all the people who I thought deserved to die. I wanted them to die when they said they did nothing to help my mother when they admitted it with no remorse. I wrote it years ago, but just remembered it this morning when I turned on the TV. I was getting breakfast... and.... and suddenly I remembered. And when I saw it..."

The sound of a car backfiring in the distance makes her jump, but then her eyes close as she shakes her head as if admonishing herself. Her eyes open slowly and the pale blues stare at nothing.

"What if someone found this?" she asks although I don't know if she actually wants me to answer.

"It's in your hands," I tell her with strained frustration.

The huff she lets out is short and full of bitterness. Shoving the paper into her purse, she keeps going, keeps letting her emotions get the better of her.

"I've literally gone crazy." She wipes at her eyes although she doesn't dare cry. "I just don't understand. It's three in a row, like a fucking checklist." The anger comes out before she breathes in deep and says softly, "That's not a coincidence."

Spearing her fingers in her hair, she grips onto the roots at her temple. Her shoulders are hunched, and she looks worse now than she did years ago. "It's not a coincidence," she says quietly and her voice is shaky.

It looks bad. It looks really fucking bad. I can see why she'd be freaked out, but this isn't the way she should have handled it.

I can hear her breathe in sharply as I lay a hand on her shoulder, but I make sure to keep my touch gentle, and she slowly melts. Every bit of her is breaking down.

She licks her lower lip and struggles to look me in the eye as she tells me, "Ever since they found him..."

She trails off and rolls her eyes although sadness and guilt even, mar her expression.

"Calm down," I tell her as she takes in a breath. "You're all right." I try to pull her in close to me, to be close to her like I was a few nights ago, but she pulls away enough that my hands fall from her.

She looks me in the eyes as she confesses, "Ever since that night, I've had these nightmares... My mom..." She takes in a shaky breath.

"You need to sleep and eat and let it all go, Chloe." I hold her gaze as I take a step closer to her, willing her to let it go. "People die."

"They're being killed," she replies forcefully, although her bottom lip wobbles. Her eyes dart from me to the door as she takes a half step back. "I dreamed of her last night," she whispers darkly. "With Tamra. And the others before."

Letting out a breath, I straighten my back and run a hand through my hair. Behind the butcher's is a mechanic shop and I stare at a patch of rust on an old beat-up hood as a wind gust blows by and the heat lets up for a moment.

"You didn't do this," I tell her without looking at her.

"I feel like I'm going crazy," she says in a sad voice that forces me to look at her. Her doe eyes reach mine. "Truly crazy, Sebastian."

"You're scared and searching for meaning where

there is none," I tell her, hoping she'll just drop it already.

"I don't know what to think, but it's not--"

"A coincidence?" I cut her off, staring into her eyes and forcing her to let it go. "It is. That's all this is."

Her head wavers with the smallest of shakes and she looks at me bewildered. "But even you said the cops would think--"

"Jesus," I cut her off again and run a hand down my face. "Is that what got to you?" I ask her, tilting my head and staring at her like she should know better. I can feel my brow furrow as she struggles to come up with an answer.

"Chloe, you can't be doing this. You need to sleep-"

"I did!" she protests.

"More than one night," I add. "And you need to eat. You need to take care of yourself and stop worrying about those assholes."

She lifts her hand up to her shoulder and lets her thumb drag along the collar of her shirt as she looks out onto the mechanic's shop. "It's just a coincidence?" she asks me, although it sounds more like a hopeful statement. I wait until her eyes are on me to tell her, "Yeah, you're just tired, Chlo."

She holds my gaze for a second and I swear if it had been a second longer, I would have had to look away.

"I'm sorry," she says with another shake of her head.

Biting down on her bottom lip she looks away from me and says, "I didn't mean to come here and..."

"You definitely shouldn't have come here," I tell her with a seriousness that makes her flinch.

"I..." she starts to respond and then corrects herself, "I said I was sorry." The instant the words slip from her, I can feel her walls start to go up. For a moment I had her, but I'll be damned, I don't want to lose it. Not again.

"Come have lunch with me." I don't offer her an out or a chance to turn me down. Feeling the heat get to me from the direct sun, I wipe my hand down the back of my neck. "You need to eat anyway."

"I don't know that I should," she tells me although her words come out as if she's asking a question.

A huff of disbelief leaves me. "So, you think it's okay to come here and talk to me about people being murdered?" I wait for her eyes to meet mine before I continue. "But going out to lunch is where you draw the line?" I let my expression show a bit of disappointment, even a little sadness. She's always been a sucker for that.

"I'm sorry." Her expression shifts to one of sympathy as she says, "I didn't mean--"

"I know what you meant," I tell her and splay my hand on the small of her back, giving the shop one more look before guiding Chloe around the building to the front parking lot. "You need to eat."

CHLOE

This diner isn't remarkable, but the food is. I think it's all the salt they put on everything. They even put it on the pizza.

Even though it's my favorite place to eat, I'm surprised I was able to eat anything at all.

The fear and paranoia are embarrassing. I'm fucking embarrassed I got so worked up this morning. It's just... finding that list and the nightmares really got to me. I felt like I was drowning in a childish fear that still has its claws rooted deep in my thoughts.

The fear faded to uneasiness when Sebastian talked me down. Just being around him makes me feel safe and protected. If I could be with him always, I would. Because he settles something deep down inside of me. He makes me crave more. More from life, but also more from him.

A different kind of nervousness took over the moment I got into his car. The soft leather was something I didn't expect. The hum of the air conditioner and the occasional clearing of Sebastian's throat were the only noises the entire ride.

This morning, I had to tell someone and he's my only someone, even if that's a pathetic truth. I didn't think twice. He didn't answer his phone, so I went to where I knew he'd be. It made every bit of sense to me at the time.

Until I slipped into his car and was engulfed in his scent. Until I peeked at him as he drove his car with an air of dominance and authority.

In a room with other people, or even in a room I'm used to being in, Sebastian is still the boy who kissed me. But alone, in his car, something changed. And suddenly I lost my voice along with every thought I ever had, except for the dirty ones that crept up late at night about Sebastian doing more than just kissing me.

Today has been nothing but a series of fucked up thoughts running wild in my head.

"What's on your mind, Chloe Rose?" His deep, rough voice breaks into my thoughts and I take my time reaching for another fry, carefully taking a bite before answering him.

"Just wondering about how much can change in a single day."

I can feel the heat rise up my chest and to my

cheeks, all the way to my hairline as he leans forward, his broad shoulders stretching out the t-shirt as he tells me, "I would swear you were thinking about something else."

His steely blue eyes seize all my attention and hold me accountable. I can barely breathe, but he doesn't need the confirmation. He's plenty full of himself already, so I simply eat the rest of the fry and shrug. I ignore the butterflies and the desire to push him for more of that teasing side of him. This is the part of his personality I've craved, but I don't want to appear desperate or say something stupid. I don't want to ruin it. I can barely believe I'm here with him. I don't even want to think about it for too long; I'm afraid if I do, it'll all go away.

His cocky half smirk is what makes me look anywhere but at him as I try to remember how I ended up here with him.

Thoughts that I wish I hadn't tried to return to.

Remembering when my mother died, how I felt the same way. Afraid and paranoid. I felt like no one understood why I was so completely distraught. The mix of emotions never felt right, and I never had any control over them. They hit me relentlessly, like the constant blow of boughs as I was forced to run through trees in a forest. Swiping at me, scratching me, taking me by surprise. I was only a girl, but old enough to remember, old enough to know I could have done something.

"I thought I was done with all this," I tell him absently.

"How's that?" Sebastian asks me with his brow furrowed and a look in his eyes that's compassionate and curious. This is how I imagined he'd look when I read those texts all that time ago. It was only an image conjured in my head because I'd never seen anything of him other than the hard, dangerous boy he wanted everyone to see.

"Do you really want to know?" I question him, the uneasiness returning. He nods his head once and I figure, why not? I have no one to talk to and after this, I'm not sure he'll even talk to me again. So why not let it all out?

"I thought I was over feeling like this..." Before I can finish, the air conditioner blows across my skin from above me just then, and a flow of goosebumps trails down my arm and shoulders making me wish I hadn't picked this seat.

"You want to switch spots?" Sebastian asks and again, I'm surprised he would ask me that.

I gently shake my head and try to recall what I was thinking only seconds ago. Before Sebastian destroyed my thoughts again with a mere five words. He's good at that.

Clearing my throat, I stare down at the half-eaten

pile of fries and remember the gut-wrenching feeling and sickness of what's to come. The living in fear and agony part. Oh yes, that's what he took my mind from.

"I thought I'd gotten over this feeling of being in constant state of fear and guilt." I don't look at him as I speak this time. If I do, I'm not certain that my mind will stay on course. "Even after you..." I don't mention what he did, and my gaze almost darts up to meet his eyes, but instead, they fall on his lips. "Even after school let out that year," I say, choosing to settle on the time rather than the action we both know I'm referring to. "Even then, at night there was this feeling, but it drifted away. And then when my uncle died, I was just angry." My voice raises at the thought, my breathing coming in faster.

Sitting back into my seat, I look at him and feel as if I should feel ashamed, but I'm not.

"Angry?" he questions.

"Yeah. I was angry. It wasn't fair that I was stuck here." Emotions threaten to come up at my admission. I loved my uncle and he'd passed only two years ago, right before I graduated high school. I was old enough to take the shit debt he left behind. "I know it's not his fault; he wanted better for me..."

I don't finish that line of thinking. "The point is, I thought I was done with all of this. For the first time in so long, I was fine."

"You were relying on yourself. So, of course, you

were fine." Sebastian sounds confident in his response, but he doesn't get it. Parts of me are so thoroughly broken that even the idea I have to rely on myself is horrifying. Rebecca used to say it was understandable after the trauma I'd been through. What she called trauma, I just called my childhood. No wonder I turned to books and writing to help me cope. Getting lost in my stories was a lot more enjoyable than facing reality.

"Everyone needs someone," I answer him, holding his gaze and praying he can feel what I mean. That he can know how deeply settled I am in that decision.

"You didn't have a someone, and you were fine."

I almost answer him with, I didn't say everyone *deserves* someone. Almost. But I decide to swallow it down. I sure as hell don't want his pity.

The ping of my phone distracts me from the conversation. Sebastian's here with me, so it must be Angie. Pulling it out, I see I'm right.

Where the hell are you? Stop being a bitch and answer me!

Angie certainly has a way with words.

I'm not coming in. I send her the response and then think better of it and add, *I'm sorry. I'm just not feeling all that well today.*

Before she can reply, I silence my phone and slip it back into my purse. She wouldn't understand. She'd think I'm crazy. Shit, I think I'm crazy. My heart beats a little faster at remembering the pure fear that ran through me when I saw Tamra died. My name was on the bottom of that list. If someone else made a list like mine, would my name be on theirs too?

The chill from the air conditioner comes back and I let my head fall back with my eyes closed, suppressing the urge to feel anything at all. I'd rather be numb to it all. Goosebumps prick along my skin once again, slowly this time. It's just the chill, I tell myself. It's definitely from the air conditioner.

"Who's that?"

Sebastian's question distracts me from my thoughts and I open my eyes slowly to tell him, "Nobody."

"So, nobody texted you?" Sebastian asks with what feels like a touch of jealousy. I'm ashamed by the way my body reacts. I feel a heat that swells from the pit of my stomach, rising up but also moving lower. Forcing a small smile to my lips, I answer him, "Just a friend."

When his expression doesn't change, I roll my eyes at him and say, "I finally got one of those." My answer is pitiful, but I own it. I don't care that I'm a loner who prefers books and writing and hiding away in my stories. Books are cheap, and the people in them are better than the ones I have left here.

He looks like he's going to say something else, but he doesn't. He finishes his drink and then reaches for his wallet.

"I can buy lunch," I offer. "After all, I kind of ruined your day." He cocks a brow and doesn't answer me.

Instead he puts some cash down on the table, more than enough to pay for both of us.

"I said I can get this one," I tell him and reach for the cash to shove it back to him, but he snatches my wrist. Electricity shoots through me, the desire returning with a blazing force.

He releases me slowly and I bring my wrist back to me, staring at it as if it's been singed. I'm reeling in the shivers that flow through my body.

"I pay," is all he says, with a forcefulness that spikes desire through me. I can't break his gaze, I can't speak.

"I want to," he adds in a gentler tone.

"How do you do this to me?" I ask him, but then I think of a different question. "Why are you doing this?"

"Because I want to." He uses the same intensity as before, but somehow his words come out softer, almost comforting. The tension is thick between us and I wonder if he feels the same pull I do. "Why did you come to see me?" he asks me, and the question breaks the spell, my eyes falling to the table and the realization that the lunch is over. That this moment is only temporary, just like Sebastian's presence in my life.

"Because I wanted to," I offer him a similar response, shrugging and then pulling up the baggy sleeves to my t-shirt. How is it that hours have passed, and I've only just now realized I'm in my pajamas? I didn't even bother to put on mascara. I always put on mascara, I look so much younger without it.

"Are you going to tell me why you're doing this?" I ask him again, feeling irritated by everything, especially my reaction to the series of events that happened today.

"I just wanted to have a nice meal with you." Hearing those words from him makes me smile and let out a short laugh. My mirth doesn't wane when he looks at me with confusion, instead, it only makes me grin harder. Maybe I truly am crazy.

"What'd I say?" he asks, and I just shake my head, taking a peek at him while lowering my lips to have a sip of Coke from the straw.

I let the bubbling fizz relax me and then straighten myself to tell him, "Just the thought of you having a nice lunch and then heading off to your nine-to-five job."

The charming grin grows on his face, revealing his perfect white teeth. "Don't you know I'm a hardworking, blue-collar type of man?"

I hold his gaze and keep my smile in place as I tell him, "I know who you are, Sebastian Black."

My taunting doesn't get me the reaction I'm after. Instead, he slips his mask back into place, hiding from me.

My next breath is accompanied by a long stretch and then I take another drink. A coldness sets in between us. I can feel it coming. It used to come so often when we were forced to be together. The moment he knew he'd let me in, he'd shut it down.

I should have known better than to think it would last. Maybe I didn't think it would, but I sure as fuck want it to.

"Something is truly wrong with me," I speak the thought without conscious consent.

"You're a product of your environment," Sebastian answers me. He sinks back against the booth and stares at me long and hard. The fake, thin leather protests as he watches the front door.

"I should get home," I tell him, so we can end whatever this moment has been. "I'm sorry I came and…. decided to be crazy and vent to you."

"I'm not." He answers me the same way he did with paying for lunch. No nonsense, no bullshit. And the same response flows through my body. For years, in school and up till the day my uncle died, I wanted him to be like this with me. To just talk to me.

"Be careful what you say at the shop though," he tells me and then adds, "people listen." The tone in which he says it brings an uneasy feeling over me and with a tightness in my throat, I start to tell him I'm sorry, but he cuts me off.

"Just so you know for next time." The softness to him, it does something to me I can't explain. *Next time.* As if I could have this moment again with him.

"You're different," I marvel at the revelation out loud.

"I'm not the one who's different."

"What do you mean?" I search his eyes for answers, wanting to know how he meant me to take that statement. *Needing* to know.

"Does it matter?"

"I don't know what matters anymore."

"What do you know, Chloe Rose?"

The way he asks it, or maybe it's just my own thoughts, but it feels like the way he asks it is so much dirtier than what he actually asked.

"I know I should go to work or go home." Neither of those options sounds appealing, but both are true.

"It'll already be two by the time you get to work," he says and shakes his head, "don't bother."

"Home it is then," I say, easily conceding, and reaching for my purse as I scoot out of the booth to stand. "Thank you for lunch," I tell him and then add, "I can walk since it's--"

"Let me take you home." He doesn't look me in the eyes when he gives the command, he doesn't even look at me. It's clearly non-negotiable, so I don't bother objecting.

The drive back to my place is even worse than the drive to the diner. Thankfully, it only takes about four minutes. And two of those were spent at a red light.

"I really could have walked," I tell him as I slip out of

his car. He opened his door first, intent on getting out rather than just dropping me off, so I walk a little quicker, eager to get to my front door first and cut him off there. I just want to be alone for a while. I want to hide away if I can. I need to process everything, but Sebastian has a way of bringing me out of my hiding place and showing me more of this world that makes me want to risk living.

"Should I come in and look around?" he asks as his car keys dangle from his hand. He stands in front of me expectantly, but I can't give him that.

"I'd prefer it if you didn't." The moment I unlock the door and turn around, I block the doorway and put a hand on the doorknob. It's only open wide enough for me to stand in the gap comfortably. "I think I need to decompress; today's been a lot to handle."

He cocks a brow at me in that way I like. "You wouldn't lock me out, would you?"

The way he asks makes me smirk, which slowly shifts into a genuine smile as I consider him. He's so tall, so much taller than how he is in my thoughts. And his shoulders, so wide. He could protect me from anything. That pull to him is so strong it's scary. But Sebastian himself doesn't scare me, not in the least. He never has. It's the power he has over me that's terrifying. "I would... but if you asked to come in, I'd let you."

My answer puts a smile on his face that matches mine. "See? I told you, you're different."

I huff a laugh, shaking my head. I'm not so sure that I'm different. It's more like I'm letting him see more of me. That's not the same thing.

He leans in close as I fail to summon a response, so close that I know exactly what he would want if I didn't lock him out tonight. I'm in over my head with him, hot and bothered and wanting the same thing he does.

I need to get away from this city more than ever.

"Get some sleep then," he says softly, in a deep, rugged tone when my eyes meet his. The carnal need that burns in his gaze sets my body on fire. I'm still standing there, watching him walk away when I can finally breathe again.

What is he doing to me?

The feeling deep in my gut, the one that used to be constantly present, still lingers as I walk up the stairs. Something is telling me it's not all right, it's not a coincidence. But that something is quieted by the thoughts of Sebastian and the idea that if it's not all right, I can run to him. It brings out a strength in me I desperately need. He does that to me. And I find it hard not to be drawn to him even more because of it, my stupid heart especially. He's been good at hurting it in the past, but it still wants more of him.

SEBASTIAN

The second her door closed, I felt eyes on the back of my head. I could feel someone watching. But when I turned around, there wasn't a single soul in sight. No neighbors on their porch, no kids playing in the street.

Fuck, I'm just as paranoid as she is. The sound of my boots slapping on the cement stairs pounds as hard as my pulse does in my ears.

When I get in my car, I lock the doors but don't turn the key in the ignition. Not just yet. The light in her bedroom isn't on and I wait, staring at the curtains until the soft yellow glow floods the window. Even though dusk hasn't hinted at its arrival, I can still see she's turned on the light.

I'm tired as fuck. I couldn't sleep last night, and I don't have a clue when I'll finally be able to rest easy again. The image of Chloe in my bed soothes the beast inside me. The caged animal that needs to be released. If she was next to me, in my arms and in my bed, I'd sleep then.

I pick up my phone and call Carter, needing some relief tonight and wondering if he'd drive by and keep a lookout for me. I don't like the way she's thinking and worse, the way she's acting. I can't risk her doing anything stupid, like telling anyone else about that list.

The phone rings. And rings. An unsettling feeling in my gut churns until he picks up. I'm reminded that his mom's doing worse and worse. One day he'll answer and tell me she's gone. I fucking dread that day. The cancer's been eating at her for two years now; she doesn't look like herself anymore with all the weight she's lost. She can't go anywhere without getting winded. It's only a matter of time at this point.

"Hey man, I'm having a rough time. I was just about to call you."

"What's going on?" I ask him, feeling guilty that I forgot the shit he's going through.

There's silence for a long time before he tells me, "It's just getting harder."

"You all right?"

I can hear him swallow before he replies, "As all right as I can be." I forget what it's like to have a family, let alone what it would be like to watch someone you love to slowly die in front of you. "You need me to do anything?" I ask him.

Again, there's only silence.

"Nah," he says. "What is it you needed?"

With his question, comes a beep signaling I've received a text and instantly I think it's Chloe. Looking up and watching as the light goes off and the window loses its light, I answer him, "It was just a passing thought, it doesn't matter."

"You sure?"

"Yeah," I answer him. "But if you need anything, let me know. I got you."

I don't rush getting off the phone with Carter, but he does, ending the call right then with the sound of his father yelling in the background. My heart goes out to the kid.

More than a time or two I've thought about showing his dad what it's like to have someone take out their anger and fear on a man, but I don't know if Carter would forgive me for stepping in. Or whether it would just make things worse on him. His family is his. It's what he told me when I suggested it once. I never want to get between him and his family. Never. No matter how fucked up they are.

The second the line goes dead, I check my text messages, but the message isn't from her.

Are you going back on your word?

I read the text from the unknown number with a

mix of anger and fear coloring my consciousness as I stare at the words.

I turn the key in the ignition, although I know I'll be back tonight once the sun has set. I'm dead set on staying right here tonight. Right in front of her house until the early morning's passed. I don't need to sleep. I can sleep when I'm dead.

I answer, *No, I understand what I have to do. She's staying out of it. She doesn't know.*

The unknown number replies, *Good. I'd hate for you to find out what would happen if you go back on your word.*

CHLOE

"*Y*ou didn't come visit me on my birthday."

I hear my mom's voice in the pitch black of my dream. The darkness spreads all around me. I can't see.

"I missed you," she says but her voice sounds closer this time and it echoes all around me. The only other sounds are my chaotic breathing and the pounding of my heart as fear filters into my blood. Every pulse feels harder and forces the desperation to get out of here to climb high into my throat.

Run.

I try to run; I try to scream. But I can't.

Open your eyes. Wake up!

I wish I could obey my own pleas.

Slowly my eyes open, but I'm not in my bed. I'm in the alley on Park Street. I swear I feel tears on my face. My throat is raw from hours of screaming. My nails are broken and there's blood everywhere. The metallic scent of it, the feel of it dried but still sticky and wet in other places over my skin, it's all I can smell and feel.

My body is so heavy.

"Why didn't you come visit me?" My mother's voice taunts me as I try to lift my head.

My body's heavy, lying on the ground. My cheek is flat against the cold, hard asphalt.

"I wanted to sing you a lullaby, baby girl. I miss being your mama." I feel fresh tears start.

"Please don't," I whimper where I am. The pain flows as freely as the fear of seeing her again. I wish I could run.

"So, did I, baby girl," my mother responds to my unspoken thoughts. "Or for someone to help me," she adds.

I hear footsteps behind me and my heart pounds harder and faster. The adrenaline in my body is useless.

On instinct, I scream for help, but my voice is so quiet.

"No one can hear you, baby girl." She's closer. My body trembles and I try so hard to move, but not a single limb obeys. I try my fingers. One by one, please. Please move, but nothing moves. I'm cemented where I am.

"Well, maybe they can, but they don't listen."

The chill from the night air gets colder as a darker shadow covers my body. She's behind me now. I try to swallow, so I can clear my throat and beg her, but it's pointless.

"It's time for your lullaby," she threatens.

"I promise I'll sleep." My words come out as a strangled plea. I remember the way the heavy base of the glass vodka

bottle landed against my temple. She didn't sing it like this, so calmly. It started out this way though. And once she started, she never stopped. Not until I was unconscious. She knew when I was pretending. She always knew.

"Go to sleep," she sings to me in a gravelly voice, dry and slurred from drinking, "go to sleep, lit-tle Chlo-e."

Tears stream down my cheeks.

"Close your eyes, rest your head."

Remembering how she beat me furiously with the bottle.

She drags her finger across my skin, trailing along the curve where my neck meets my shoulders. Her nail is jagged and slick with fresh blood. Pulling my hair behind my neck so she can whisper in my ear, she finishes the lullaby, "It's time for bed."

SEBASTIAN

I debate on sending the text. I'm staring at the phone in my hand like I'm back in high school.

You didn't go to work today either?

The words stay right where they are, waiting for me to send them. I know she's all right; no one's approached her, no one's messaged her. Although, she hasn't left the house since I walked her to her door. Not two nights ago, not last night and she called out from work again this morning.

I know she's in there. I've been watching every inch of that place.

"Mr. Black." A man's deep voice disrupts me from my thoughts. Sitting at the lone desk in the back room of the shop, I can see him through the open door. He's standing in the front of the butcher shop, peeking behind the counter, and trying to get a look into the kitchen.

"Officer Harold," I answer him in a monotone and slip the phone into my pocket. I just got in and didn't see his car in the lot. But I didn't check for it either. I didn't do anything except worry about leaving Chloe Rose alone in that house. She's getting to me even worse than she did back in high school.

All I can do is think about her, and that's a mistake. For both of us.

"What can I do for you?" I ask him as I walk out of the back and head straight toward him. As I cross my arms, I make a mental note of who all's in here. Eddie's behind the front counter and watching everything, although he's pretending to go through the weekly invoices. I don't know why he bothers putting up a front. Officer Harold is in Romano's back pocket and Eddie knows that. As does everyone else who's working in the back.

So that means Romano sent him, or this is a test.

Either way, I don't care for it. Other than Eddie, I don't think anyone else is here yet. Which could be bad news for Eddie if this goes south.

"Have you heard about the recent killing spree?" he asks me and gestures to one of the two small tables in this place. They're circular with peeling, flaking vinyl on the top and thin metal legs that match the rickety chairs. They're dated and not meant to keep people wanting to stay. Most of the people who come in here pick up their packages and leave. Those who decide they want to hang around often change their minds as quickly as they can sit their asses down in these spindly seats.

"Killings?" I question him like I haven't thought much about it. The sound of the metal feet of the chair dragging across the floor makes Eddie cringe as he peeks up from scratching his pencil on the notepad. "I know Tamra Stetson was shot and killed, I heard about that the other day."

"Tamra and before her, Barry Jones, a few days before him a girl named Amber Talbott was found dead." Officer Harold doesn't sit like I do. Instead, he remains standing. Fucking prick.

I push back the chair and spread my legs wide as I sit back and shrug. "I only know what you know," I offer him, and he gives me a smug smirk.

"And what is it that you think I know?" he taunts me, sucking his teeth and keeping his back to Eddie. Eddie doesn't hide the fact he's watching.

Again, I shrug and say, "Whatever's in the paper and on the news."

It's quiet for a moment. Not a sound from anything. Not the air conditioner, not the cars outside. Nothing as he watches me, looking over my expression. I keep it easy and relaxed. It's something I worked hard to accomplish. You never let them see a damn thing from you. Carter said his dad taught him that once. That you don't give anyone anything. It's the one thing Carter taught me that's helped me survive longer than I would have otherwise.

"And what about your girl, Chloe?" Officer Harold asks me, and Eddie stops jotting on his pad. The scratching of the pencil halts and my heart pounds heaviy. I can feel my lips twitching on my face to pull down into a scowl and the need for my forehead to show a sharp crease.

I want to rip out his throat for even mentioning her name. I wish I could see her right now. That I could see she's safe and ensure they'll leave her out of this. Adrenaline pumps hard in my blood knowing she's involved now, but she did that to herself when she came here. Fuck, I wish I could take it back.

I can protect her though. I *will* protect her; I'll make this right.

"Chloe Rose?" I say her name and force my face to soften, to stay casual wondering how the best way to play this would be. I rub the stubble on my chin and look past him. "What about her?"

"Why did you go to see her?" he asks me. Anxiety races through me. She's always flown under the radar. Gorgeous and tempting, but no one's paid her any mind. No one wants to deal with the sad girl who's stuck here with no one and nothing. Now she's a person of interest, all because of me.

"She came to see me," I correct him.

"That's not what I heard." My pulse pounds at my temples. And again, I struggle to keep my composure. I feel my throat get tight as I swallow.

Letting out a low sigh, I exaggerate. "A few nights ago, she was walking home." I meet his eyes to add, "Alone. And the streetlight went out. Spooked her some."

His eyes stay hard as I sniff and shrug my shoulders. "She wanted some company. I checked out her place. I don't know if you know this, officer, but someone broke into her house a while back."

His eyes narrow; I know damn well that he knows what I did. I had to tell Romano, who tells Officer Harold when he doesn't have to go searching for a killer. Problem is, Romano doesn't know who's doing these killings. Romano should know if I had something to do with it, I'd tell him. The fact that Officer Harold is here is telling. The uneasiness flows through me the more I think about it.

I shrug. "I guess she liked that I was willing to give her some company." I tilt my hips up some, implying a little more happened. "I liked it too."

"So, this has nothing to do with Tamra Stetson or the killing spree?" he asks me and sucks his teeth again, but his demeanor has changed. No longer on the attack, instead he's desperate for a lead.

"It's freaking Chloe out some, being alone and watching these girls turning up dead... which is only helping me get laid. But I don't know shit that could help you."

"Just to clarify." The good officer puts both hands on the table and leans forward, getting so close I can see where he nicked his chin when he was shaving. "For everyone," he adds, although the heavy implication is that Romano will hear about whatever I say. I already know that though. This little visit was obviously triggered by Chloe running in here the other day. I know damn well that Romano doesn't know shit, and neither does this prick.

"Whatever you want to know," I say and stare him dead in his eyes, feeling the tension rise.

"You don't know anything?" His eyes search mine as I answer him, "Not a damn thing."

My heart beats chaotically and I swear if he could hear, he'd know I'm lying.

Sniffing and standing straight, Harold fixes his shirt, tucking it back in. "If you hear anything..." he says even though he's already walking out. With his back to me, he doesn't bother to give any parting words. Only the sound of the bells bids him farewell.

"What's up his ass?" I ask Eddie even though my eyes are on the glass door as it closes behind him.

After a moment with no response, I look over at Eddie, but he's already gone. The notepad remains on the counter, the top piece ripped off.

There are enemies everywhere. Every step of the way.

The deeper I get with Romano, the less likely it is I'll ever have a chance to leave.

CHLOE

They feel so real. That's why I can't shake them.

The nightmares are something I was used to when I hadn't come to terms with the reality.

My mother's gone.

She died years ago.

I remind myself once again and blow across the top of the full cup of tea in my hands, but it's no longer hot, it's barely lukewarm. I've only just now realized I must have been holding it for a while without even taking a single sip. I'm slow to set the cup down on the end table and then reach for the blanket. My fingers grip on to the soft woven fabric like it can save me. Just as I used to think when I was a child.

My mother's gone.

She died years ago.

It was hard to say the words back then, but I have to keep saying them now.

Not because I don't believe them, but because every time I fall asleep now, she's there, haunting me and saying things that scare me. Things she knows would put true fear into my heart. She's reminding me of memories I've long buried.

She's angry and wants revenge for what happened. I can feel it. Her killer joining her six feet in the dirt isn't enough justice. She's starved for more. A taste of his blood wasn't enough.

When I wake up breathless and terrified by how realistic the dreams are, I can feel the weight of her hand gripping my arm, but no sane person would believe me. I would just sound crazy.

I'm going crazy. I know that's what they'd say and as I pull my knees into my chest on the sofa, I struggle to deny it. I'm fucking insane.

All I can think, is that whatever Sebastian gave me is fucking with my head. I can't sleep without seeing her, without *feeling* her. I swear the scratch on the back of my neck is from her.

I don't want to go to sleep. I only took the sweets, as Sebastian calls it, that one time, but I've been so fucked up since then. Although, so much more has happened since then too.

My fingers press into my tired eyes, feeling the burning need to sleep and I remember how I woke up last night, sweating, crying, my throat raw as if I'd been screaming. I prayed like I'd never prayed before and when I whispered for someone to help me, I felt the coldness of her presence. As the chill traveled up my spine, I swear I heard my mother whisper, "I am."

A sudden knock at the door has my heart galloping in my chest. Two days of not sleeping but also not knowing what to do has left me jolting at every sudden sound.

"Chlo," I hear Sebastian's voice call out through the front door and he knocks again as he says, "Open up."

Just hearing his voice is calming, and I easily swing my legs down and listen to my bare feet pad across the floor as I go to unlock the door and let him in.

I swing open the door without even looking in the small mirror in the hall to see if I look presentable. I'm sure I look like hell, and I wouldn't keep him waiting, so it doesn't matter anyway.

With his hand still raised to knock again, we both stand there for a moment, waiting for the other to say something. I swallow thickly, feeling the nervousness rise up again. He's never taken so long to say anything before.

"You look like you're ready for me to drag you to bed," he finally tells me and then steps inside, not waiting for me to invite him in.

"If you're lucky, I'd let you." I try to make it sound like a joke, but at this point, I would. "I feel like I'm going to fall over," I tell him groggily and turn my back on him to saunter back to the living room, but he grabs my wrist as he kicks the door shut behind him.

It closes with a click.

"What?" I ask him, staring pointedly where his fingers are wrapped possessively around my wrist. "I wasn't serious. You aren't dragging me anywhere."

Keeping my face deadpan, he cracks a smile and then I mirror his, a small simper of a smile, but it doesn't reflect anything that I feel.

"You okay?" he asks me.

Blowing a lock of hair away from my face and straightening the strap of the tank top on my shoulder I nod and ask, "What's going on?" No matter how much I want to tell someone about my nightmares, I refuse to speak the words out loud. It would only make me sound unhinged.

"The cops wanted to know why I came to see you."

Cops. That was the last thing I wanted to hear. My stomach drops, as does my gaze and I pick under my nails to distract myself.

"How would they even know?" I ask him without thinking, but if I'd just let it sink in for one second, I'd know better. *Everyone here is crooked, everyone knows everything.* It was the only good advice my mother ever gave me. *If you keep that in mind, you'll be all right.*

"Ignore me," I tell him absently and rub the tiredness from my eyes as I walk to the sofa. I plunk back down into my cozy seat and pull the throw blanket around me again.

When I peek up at Sebastian, he's eyeing me with a look I can't place. "What did you tell them?" I ask him to get the attention away from me.

"Well, I had to tell a white lie."

"What did you say?" I whisper and fight off the yawn that threatens.

"I told them you meant something to me and I was just checking in on you."

It's quiet for a moment as I take in his words. I have to remind myself of what he said. Me meaning anything to him is a white lie. The thought makes my fingers ball into a fist under the blanket.

"Okay," is all I give him as I sit there, with my neck craned so I can stare up at him as he stands in front of me.

"And now they think we may be a thing." His eyes assess me, and if I wasn't so tired, I would blush, practically ignite like I've done before. But right now, all I can think is how he said it was a white lie.

I almost ask him what a white lie means, so he can tell me to my face in blunt terms that I don't mean anything to him. Instead, I just ignore it all and focus on a pounding ache that grows in my temple.

"What's in that stuff you gave me?" I ask him a question that's been nagging at the back of my head.

"Nothing serious." His forehead creases as he answers me. "Why?"

"It feels serious to me," I tell him. although my heart beats rapidly, begging me not to push him away with my insanity.

The moment passes, and with the silence, the tension grows.

"What happened?" he asks me. "Are you sick?" The concern in his voice is so genuine that I nearly tell him to be careful, that everyone will see that I mean something to him. But the spite and jabs from his white lie comment mean nothing to me right now.

He's here. He's listening to me. Whether he realizes it or not, I know I mean something to him. So, I couldn't care less if that's what the cops think. I couldn't care less about people running their mouths or any of that right now.

There's only one thing haunting me at this moment.

"I'm just..." I trail off and swallow thickly, burying the words in my throat.

"When's the last time you took it?" he pushes for more information as he takes the seat next to me, making the old sofa groan with his weight. He sits closer to me than I sat to him last time. He's so close, I can still feel that heat that lingers on his shirt from the summer sun.

"I only took it the one night." I look up into his

steely blue eyes and watch the grey flecks mesmerize me as I add, "The night I texted you."

"You're supposed to take it every night, Chlo. It doesn't stay in your system for long."

"Are you sure?" I ask him quickly. "Because it feels like it's still in my system."

The sofa protests as I readjust in my seat to face him more and he asks, "Have you been sleeping?"

I only nod with a small frown gracing my lips as my chest tightens with worry. "I don't want to though," I whisper the confession.

"Chlo," he scolds me, immediately running the middle finger and thumb of his right hand down his temples. His large hand covers his eyes as he does it.

"Don't do that," I bite back, not hiding the sadness and disappointment at his reaction. "I'm not a child and I'm not okay." Although my voice wavers, I say the words as strongly as I can.

He lets out a heavy breath as his hand drops to his side and my eyes plead with him to understand.

"I'm afraid. I'm dreaming these things..." I gulp down the confession and settle on a simple truth as I conclude, "and it's not okay. I think it's what you gave me."

"You think the sweets has something to do with what you're dreaming about?" he asks me, and I can only nod with a tension in my stomach that threatens to make me sick. "Tell me," he says, and his command is soft and comforting. As if confiding in him will make it all go away. "Tell me what's got you worked up like this."

"It's my mother," I tell him and struggle to confess to him that every time I drift to sleep, I relive the hell that existed before she died. Every memory I've shut away and buried with her is back. "I feel crazy because the nightmares are so real." I can feel myself breaking down and the moment Sebastian notices, both of his hands are on me. One on my thigh, rubbing back and forth and the other on my shoulder. I'm in a sleep shirt that comes down to my knees, my legs covered by the blanket. His right hand though is touching my bare skin. The rough pad of his thumb rubs soothing circles against my collarbone and I lean into it. I've never felt the need to be touched so gently before. The need to be held.

If I had even a hint that he'd still respect me after, I'd climb into his lap right now.

"It's all right." His voice is strong, but also frustrated and it reminds me of that day back in high school. He's barely keeping it together as he takes me in.

"I'm sorry." I don't know what else to do other than apologize. "I don't want to be this way," I plead with him to understand. "I think when I drank the--"

"It's not the sweets. It's what's going on around us. This shit is bringing up old memories. The drug is just a knockoff pharmaceutical. Most people don't even know about it. It's like any other sleep med, Chlo. A friend gave it to me to sell, but no one buys sleep meds off the street."

"You don't understand," I tell him.

"Make me understand."

I think long and hard about exactly how to explain it. It's not an old memory. These terrors are so real and lifelike, they don't leave me when I wake up. "I'm scared," is all I can say, and the confession comes out as a whisper.

"I want you to come spend the night with me," Sebastian speaks like it's a request, but it's not. I can hear it in his voice and along with the shock is something else.

Desperation.

I can't move, thinking I've misheard him. All I can do is stare into his eyes and listen to every single beat of my heart.

"It's in my best interest to keep an eye on you," he tells me slowly and then licks his lower lip. It's slow and sensual but there's something else there like he can't quite figure something out. "You look like you could use some company. It'll do us both good."

HE GIVES me five minutes to gather a few things. It hardly takes me that long as I toss my toiletries on top of a stack of folded clean clothes and grab my purse. That's it. I don't bother with anything else.

We're not driving far, but even so, the car ride is quiet in a way that absorbs my every thought. Sebastian Black... and me. Maybe one day I'll wake up and all of this will be a dream. Or maybe one day, he'll come with me and we can run away from this nightmare.

"Haven't you ever thought about leaving?" I let the internal thought wander to my lips as I rest my cheek against the car window. The hum of the engine and the gentle vibrations threaten to lure me to sleep, but I fight it.

"You don't think I want to leave too?" he asks me, taking his eyes from the road to look at me. I don't answer, I just take him in, right here at this moment. The strength that is Sebastian Black, veiled with the secret that he'd rather run away. My heart hurts for him in this instant; I always thought he ran this city and that he thrived because of it. How foolish I was. I realize that now as he tells me, "When you figure out where you're going to run to, let me know."

SEBASTIAN

I didn't even think to be embarrassed or ashamed until Chloe stopped in the foyer. All I was thinking was that I was done leaving her alone. I don't have a good feeling about any of this shit and I just want to keep her close. I never considered what she'd think of my place though. Or what she'd think of me.

"Welcome home," I tell her as I toss my keys onto the skinny kitchen counter next to the pile of unopened mail I got yesterday.

There's a sofa, a coffee table, and a TV. Nothing else in this room. It's never looked bare before, until now. It's never felt like it was lacking in any way until I see Chloe not moving from where she is.

The sofa came with throw pillows I didn't like, so I tossed them out, but there's a standard bed pillow and

117

an old blanket in a heap on the far end of the sofa. That's where Carter sleeps when he needs a place to crash.

This house is small, with only one bedroom and the kitchen is the size of a freaking dime, directly across from the living room. But I paid with cash and I own it. That's the only thing I was looking for when I knew I needed to leave my ma's old place. There was too much shit there. Too much of the past cluttering and smothering my every thought.

"Not what you expected?" I ask her dully and keep walking to the sofa to take off my shoes.

I have a nice car and nice threads for when I need them. All my cash is hidden in the floorboard under my cabinet sink. I don't spend anything I don't have to. You never know when you may need to run, and I'll have the cash for that, make no mistake about it.

"You're such a man. You could at least grab a candle at the corner store or something. Maybe hang a picture?" she suggests, and her lips pull up into a teasing smile.

She finally walks into the room, kicking off her shoes next to mine and slipping into the side of the sofa Carter usually takes. She goes to grab his blanket, but I stop her. It's weird seeing her gravitate to his things. And to want his things.

"You can have the bed," I offer her and then add, "That's Carter's stuff."

"Oh." A shyness spreads through her expression as she gently pushes it away. "Sorry," she adds and then clears her throat. "Do you have a throw for out here?" she asks.

"You like being under the covers, don't you?" I ask teasingly, and it makes her smile as she nods. I like that. I like how I can make her smile. I like that even when she's worked up and upset. When her mind is wandering to disturbing things, I can make her smile and give her something to take away the pain.

"Let me grab you the other blanket," I say as I stand up. There's a small linen closet outside of the bathroom, and I have my old blanket in there.

"I don't know that the Cross boys like me much," she tells me from the living room even though I can barely hear her in here.

I just washed the blanket the other night and I can still smell the laundry detergent as I bring it out to her. "Why would you think that?" I ask her and play dumb even though I know why she would.

"My mom was kind of into their dad once, and couldn't take a hint," she says softly, but cheers up when she sees my blanket. "Ninja Turtles?"

A huff of comforting humor leaves me as I nod.

"You aren't your mom. They know that," I say to try to ease her worries.

"Yeah, but…" she starts to say, but I shake my head and she trails off, waiting patiently to hear what I'm going to tell her. She brushes a lock of hair behind her ear and snuggles into the sofa, resting her head on the back cushion.

"I know Carter, and he likes you just fine. More than he likes most people." I focus on Carter, not his family. It wouldn't be fair to blame Chloe for her mother's mistakes. That'd be like her judging Carter for his father's actions.

"I think he's all right, too," she says softly with her eyes closed, nestling deeper into the sofa.

"I said you could sleep in the bed, Chlo," I remind her and watch as her eyes slowly open, giving me more of that soft blue mix of pale hues that look through me.

"I don't want to sleep," she tells me just above a murmur.

A sickness spreads through my chest and down to my gut, settling into a heavy pit there. "You need to sleep."

Even though my words are hard and non-negotiable, she gives me a sad smile. "No shit. I can't stay awake forever, but it feels like I'm trying."

"You don't like the sweets?" I ask her, remembering what she said about it fucking with her and making her remember shit she didn't want to. "It's just supposed to relax you. I think everything that's going on is messing with your head."

"I don't want it to happen again." Sadness slowly seeps into her eyes, but she doesn't elaborate.

"Don't want what exactly?" I ask her, and her expression falls completely as she searches my gaze.

"They're just nightmares," she whispers, and I don't know if it's more to convince herself or me.

"They come and go; you can't stop them by running yourself into the ground like this," I tell her and run my hand over the back of my head. As I do, I feel the weight of my own exhaustion taking over.

"I have Benadryl. I could go get Nyquil?" I give her some options, just hoping she'll take something. The person who gave me the sweets made it sound like it was the best thing to take to relax and sleep easy. That's the only reason I gave it to her. It worked for me and I thought it might help her. "You gotta sleep, Chlo."

"I know I do," she tells me and then readjusts her head on the cushion until she's more comfortable, but still looking at me. The look of exhaustion drives a primal need inside me to help her sleep however I can. Even if that means fucking her into my bed. The thought is only a flash in my vision of her legs wrapped around my hips, her heels digging into my ass as I pound into her. A split second of that thought has me rock hard instantly.

I want to kiss her again, but that would just complicate everything. It feels good to have someone needing you like this though. Wanting you and letting you get close.

Word is already going around. As long as I do what I'm supposed to, maybe I can have her...

"Let's go to bed," I suggest, readjusting and trying to ignore the aching need that's pressing against the zipper of my jeans. I've wanted her for so fucking long. With a quick glance at her curves hidden beneath the covers, I start wondering if she'd let me. If she needs me like I need her.

"Sebastian, tell me you didn't bring me here just so you could fuck me." Her voice is breathy, but there's a tinge of fear there. She hasn't moved from where she's sitting, but she's still as she waits for my answer.

"Why do I keep finding myself telling you that you should know better?" I expect her to flinch at my tone, or to drop the subject altogether. I don't expect her to press me, which is exactly what she does.

"So, you don't want to sleep with me?" she asks, and I don't hesitate to tell her, "I want to fuck you more than I want to breathe right now."

Chloe Rose's eyes widen and her breath hitches as my blood heats.

"But it's not why I brought you here, and you know it," I add.

I can hear her swallow as she glances at my throbbing cock. "We can just go to sleep. I'm tired too," I offer her.

I hadn't realized I was holding my breath until she nods her head. "Okay," she says, already pushing off the sofa and standing up with a yawn. "Should I bring this one too?" she asks, holding up the corner of my blanket.

"Leave it there," I answer her and start walking down the hall. I walk slowly so she knows to follow, and she does. Her footsteps are soft and hesitant.

Pulling back the sheets for her, I look over my shoulder and then nod to the left side of the bed, the farthest from the doorway where she's still standing.

She has one hand on each side of it, and in her sleep shirt, her legs are on full display. Smooth and lush. She rubs one calf against the other as she nervously waits in the doorway. "No funny business?" she asks.

"Not unless you want," I tell her, feeling the disappointment overwhelm me. I've thought about having her here for years. Literally, years. I have to stare at my nightstand as I strip out of my shirt. When I unzip my pants, I see her walk around the bed, but more importantly, I feel her eyes on me. Her lust-filled gaze doesn't see mine on hers as she nearly walks into the bed in her rush to get under the sheets. She doesn't notice how I watch her lick the seam of her lips as her gaze travels down my body.

And I'll never forget how her eyes widen and her bottom lip drops slightly for her to take a deep inhale when I kick off my pants and she sees what I have for her.

Every fucking inch of it will slide into that tight cunt of hers.

Maybe not tonight, but knowing how much she wants me, how much she's desperate for what she sees, brings a cocky smirk to my face that I can't hide.

When the sheets stop rustling and Chloe's nestled under the comforter, I ask her, "You want to be the big spoon or little spoon?"

And I'm rewarded with the sweet, sarcastic laugh I knew she'd give me.

"No spooning," she answers with the smile still firmly on her face.

"You sure?" I ask as I slip into bed beside her. "It can get a little cold, you may find yourself wanting some warmth." I cock a brow, but she's not having it. "I'm practically a heater myself. My body temperature is just a little hotter than normal."

When she laughs this time, I smile wider and set my head down on the other pillow in the bed. She rubs her eyes and then rolls over to lie on her side, facing me with both of her hands tucked under her pillow.

"You're the different one," she whispers, reminding me of the night I dropped her off at her house when she said I was different and I said it right back to her. "This wouldn't be so easy if you were still the way you were before."

I have to lick my lower lip to keep from saying

anything. She has no idea. "I guess we're both a little different, but can I tell you a secret?"

She only nods, her hair ruffling against the pillow as she does. "I've always wanted you."

With her teeth sinking into her bottom lip, she tries to stifle her smile, but she can't.

"Aw, aren't you cute when you blush?" I tease her, and I'm rewarded with a little more of a smile.

"What if we did do something?" she asks after a moment. Her breathing picks up and I can feel her nervousness.

I nearly groan from my cock leaking precum at the thought of doing *something* with her.

"What kind of something?" I ask her, doing my best to tread lightly. I get the feeling that she'd run from me and put those walls back up if I made a single misstep. I'm so eager to be inside of her, I could stumble and fall my way down a flight of stairs into fucking this up.

She shrugs and waits for me to say something.

"Is there anything you wouldn't do?" I ask her out of pure curiosity. With her hips, the image of her face down on my bed with her ass up is everything I want right now. My cock stiffens again at the thought and this time I let out a small groan.

Her eyes travel away from my gaze and downward.

"I'm sure there's a lot I wouldn't do… or maybe not," she says absently. "My friend said she liked being choked." The mention of choking catches me off guard.

Of all the things for my innocent Chloe Rose to say, that wasn't one I couldn't have guessed.

"You want me to choke you?" I ask her, not hiding my surprise.

"No!" Pushing her hand against my chest, she backpedals real quick. "You were just asking what I wouldn't want to do but I don't know what that list would be." She nestles back down as I try to think of what she needs to hear next.

I know what I want to say. I want to go through my list of all the dirty shit I want to do to her and then have her tell me where her limits are. But I'm pretty sure that'll have her jumping out of bed faster than I can finish my laundry list of how to make Chloe Rose cum harder than she ever has before.

Confusion mars my face; I can feel it in the deep crease on my forehead. "I'm getting some mixed signals here, and I don't want to fuck this up." It's such a simple thing to admit that, but as I swallow, I feel more vulnerable than I have in a long time. Probably since the day she ran from me in school, when she ran out the door and I followed her.

"I don't want to fuck it up either," she whispers and then leans in closer, pressing a small, quick kiss to my lips. Before I can deepen it, she's already pulling away. My hand was already half up, ready to spear through her hair and keep her pressed to me, but I'm too slow, too shocked that she'd make the first move.

"If we did do something, it would only be because I think I would sleep really well after," she tells me softly, watching my expression and judging my reaction.

"You love lying to me, don't you?" I ask her with a cocked brow as I stretch out, putting one arm behind her head. She lets out a small laugh but also inches closer and rests her cheek on my arm.

With her thumbnail between her teeth, she keeps her arm up between us and I don't miss how the bottom half of her body is still farther away from me.

I glance at the clock and see how late it is before taking a look back at her, nestled in my arm with her eyes closed.

"What if tonight you take from me, whatever you want?" I offer her and then say the second half of my suggestion when her eyes flutter open. "And tomorrow night, I take from you. Whatever I want." My blood pressure rises instantly at the thought of her agreeing. I'm hot and wound up and ready to make a deal with her. "Whatever you want," I add.

Her lips part and there's a sudden movement of the bed along with the comforter. "You have to squeeze your thighs together like that?" I tease her even though the very thought of her scissoring her legs right now is killing me.

"We can do that," she agrees in a single breath. Again, she inches closer, so close, but her ass is still pointed the wrong way.

"How do you want me?" I ask her and then add, "Tomorrow night when you're ready, that's how I want you to ask me too." I'm so damn hard at the thought of her asking me that I nearly lose it when she nods her head in agreement.

"So, how do I want you?" she asks, her wide doe eyes shining with a desire that must reflect my own.

With my body coursing with adrenaline at the thought of fucking her tonight, I nod my head and say, "Tell me what you want."

She turns away from me, and for a split second I think she's going to say she doesn't want to do anything, but then she brings her ass closer to mine and all that desire rises inside of me again.

She peeks over her shoulder and grabs my hand, kissing the tip of my fingers one by one as my heart beats faster and faster. "I want your hand here," she whispers and pulls down her panties while telling me, "I've never been fingered; I want you to get me off with your hand."

I don't believe her for one second, but I don't argue. I don't even consider arguing.

All I can focus on is that she's in my bed, taking off her panties and telling me she wants me to finger fuck her. I'm content getting to third base from Chloe tonight because tomorrow night I'm getting everything I want.

Planting a small kiss on her jawline, I let her move

my fingers between her legs. She's hot and already slick with arousal. Fuck, I don't know how I don't immediately cum just from grazing my fingers across her clit.

"You're so fucking wet," I tell her the second my fingertips touch her hot entrance. I force back a groan as I push my fingers inside of her. "And so tight," I comment out loud, but the next thought is whether or not I can even fit my cock inside of her. I have to work my fingers in slowly, pressing against her front wall and holding her body down as she bucks out of instinct.

Her hips tilt up and I press my thumb against her clit. Slowly she adjusts, letting me push my fingers in deeper and deeper and stroking her front wall to get those sweet sounds to spill from her lips in a strangled moan.

Her cry of pleasure is accompanied with her pushing her head back into my shoulder as her neck arches and her body begs to do the same.

I'm barely inside of her and she's already so responsive. So easy to pleasure. As her hand moves to the back of my head, her fingernails scratching as they go down my scalp, I lean forward to kiss her neck. I'm teasing and slow with each calculated kiss, nipping and biting from the sensitive part just below her ear down to the crook of her neck.

My eyes stay open the entire time as I push my

fingers deeper and deeper inside of her, working her and desperate to warm her up so she can take me.

"Fuck," she moans a muted sigh of the word. My fingers press against her front wall, rubbing hard and forcing her pleasure from her, all while keeping my thumb pressed to her clit.

Her body writhes against me as she tries to turn over, to move away, but I wrap one leg around hers and move my arm around her chest, pinning her body to mine and holding her in place. Strangled moans are all she gives me as I pump my fingers in and out of her cunt.

My touch turns ruthless as her heels slam into the bed and she frantically grabs at the sheets. She's so fucking close. "Give it to me," I command her through clenched teeth. I can't even breathe, knowing how close she is.

"Bastian," she's moaning my name as her body trembles with my relentless touch.

I've never heard anything sound so fucking perfect as Chloe Rose moaning my name.

"Say it again," I command her, and she gasps while yelling it at the same time, "Bastian, Bastian!"

I can't help rocking my hips against her, loving how she does the same, grinding her ass against me.

"I want you," I beg her, pressing my cock against her, the only shield being the thin fabric of my boxers.

I've never wanted a girl this much. I've never felt

the need to be inside of a woman like this before. I need her. I need to feel her pussy wrapped this tight around my dick. My heart races with hers as she gets closer.

"I want you," I moan again against the shell of her ear as I press my dick against her ass, searching for relief. Instantly her pussy clamps down on my fingers, tightening and spasming as she cums.

I cum violently with her. If she wasn't so preoccupied with her own climax, I'd be embarrassed that I just came in my boxers, dry humping her.

I take my hand away from her slowly, letting her sag on her side as she tries to catch her breath. I have to hide that I'm doing the same as I flip my fingers in my mouth and make sure she's watching as I suck.

"You taste sweet too," I tell her and smile wide when she blushes that much harder.

"How did that feel, Chloe Rose?" I breathe against the shell of her ear before nipping her lobe. Pride and the heat of my own orgasm roll through my chest.

"Bastian," she whispers my name as sleep finally claims her. Her body's still trembling next to mine.

"Answer the question," I say before getting up to wash my hands and get her a washcloth, but she shakes her head slightly before I leave the room, ignoring my question as she passes out in my bed.

CHLOE

*I*t's amazing what a good night of sleep can do to a person. And a good fuck for that matter.

Sebastian was right, I was just tired and needed to sleep. It all feels so stupid now, even though the uneasiness still lingers whenever I hear whispers about the recent murders.

I can still feel Sebastian inside of me. Even as Marc, my boss, gave me a ridiculous lecture about how many sick days I have left, all I could think about was how Sebastian touched me last night.

Not just touched me. There isn't a suitable word for what he did to me. How he dragged the pleasure from me in a way I didn't know could exist.

And that was just foreplay.

The memory of how his lips felt, how his hard body felt, how his hard cock felt…

My nipples harden as a shudder rolls through my body at the thought of tonight. Sebastian is handsome, classically so with a darkness that hints at danger, but last night, everything about him resembled a sex god. The way the dim light caressed his stubble, the way his lips seemed to pout and then glisten when he licked them. And his eyes swirled with a desire I imagine could never be tamed. It's more than just lust though. The more I'm around Sebastian, the more I let myself believe there's something *more* between us.

The click of the air conditioner in the office brings my gaze up to it and then to Angie, sitting in the desk chair cross-legged and on her phone. While I'm on the floor with six piles of paper as I try to organize these documents alphabetically by last name.

"Oh, my God," Ang drags out the last word as she throws her head back and stares at the ceiling in exasperation. "Can it just be five already?" She drops her gaze to me and I have to crack a smile.

"Hard day?" I taunt her, knowing she didn't do shit. We had four clients come in today. So, she checked in four people. And that's all she's done. For eight hours.

I sit upright, stretching my back. "We could switch on Monday?" I offer her, and she tilts her head.

"I don't know why you even agreed to that shit," she tells me while making a circle with her pointer finger to encompass the papers on the floor, right before going back to her phone.

Agreed? It's my job. I bite my inner cheek to keep from responding. I need my paycheck. I need to add it to my meager savings.

The thought of why I'm so desperate to save up makes my heart squeeze in my chest.

It's so I can leave and get out of here. But things have changed. That would mean leaving Sebastian and whatever it is that we have going on now.

It's odd to feel so much, so quickly. To feel that raw loss at the thought of one day getting out of here. I'm so used to feeling lonely that it didn't take much for me to feel some sort of attachment to him. Although that feeling has come and gone for years and yet every time, I know there's something between us I'd never have with anyone else.

It only took that single kiss years ago to know that.

"I say we just get out of here," Angie suggests, interrupting my thoughts.

I shrug at her suggestion. "Marc won't notice, that's for sure."

I'm not leaving this city any time soon. And whatever I have with Sebastian will more than likely be short-lived. I'm still shocked it's happening at all.

I'll be counting the days until it ends.

Even knowing that, so confidently certain it will

end, I'm still going to give myself to him tonight. I didn't question it for a moment.

I was always his to take. And that's exactly what I want. For him to be my first.

My breathing comes out shaky as I realize the clock is ticking down to that moment and I still haven't decided if I'm going to tell him or not.

"Okay, let's just get out of here." Angie hops down from her seat, letting it roll backward and carelessly slam into her desk as she slips her ridiculously high heels back on.

"Why do you even work here?" I feel the sarcastic question slip out before I can stop myself. I feel like half a bitch, but with the nerves of what I'm going to do tonight, I'm not as careful with my words as I should be.

Angie pauses for a second and then laughs, loud and unrestrained. She shrugs, slipping on the first heel and then the second. "The perv wanted to hire me," she says and looks up at me as she continues, "and I had to pay my rent."

One point for honesty, I suppose. "Fair enough." I can't argue with that. Pushing on my thighs, I force myself to stand up and stack the piles, so I can get back to filing tomorrow and not lose my place. As I'm setting a generic glass paperweight on the stack, Angie asks me if I want a ride.

My heart does a somersault, the weirdest movement as the jitters set through me. It's been like this on and off all day.

I'm going to go to Sebastian.

Sebastian Black is going to fuck me tonight. All the anxiety and nerves mix in the pit of my stomach. Maybe if I keep telling myself it's just sex, my heart will start believing it.

"I'm good; I'm going to walk." I think I do a good job at keeping the nerves out of my voice, but I have to stare at the stack instead of looking at her.

I can feel her eyes on me though, and when I peek up, looking as innocently as I can at the only woman I've ever met who owns her sexuality like she does, she asks, "You sure?"

That little place between her eyebrows is scrunched and I'm sure she can tell something's off, but I'm not telling her shit. Not. One. Word. I don't want advice; I don't want to hear stories. Worse, I don't want her to tell me the list of women he's screwed. She has a habit of doing that whenever a man's name comes up. She's a walking encyclopedia of all things sexual and provocative.

"Yeah, I'm good," I tell her nonchalantly, and her expression tells me that she isn't buying any of it, but she doesn't ask again. She grips the doorway once, looking between the pile of papers I refuse to take my eyes from and then back up to my face.

"See you tomorrow then?" she asks and then adds, "You're not going to take another mini vacay, right?"

The smile she gets from me is genuine. "Your concern is adorable," I tell her and roll my eyes before adding, "but no, I'll see you tomorrow."

"All right, sweet cheeks," she says while tapping the doorway, "See you in the morning."

"Have a good night, Buttercup," I tell her and then scrunch my nose at Buttercup. I could have come up with something better, but the more I let it sit, the more I like it.

I listen to her heels as she walks out and then immediately grab my bag and head out the back, rather than the front. The stairwell is all concrete steps down the back, which is why no one ever leaves this way, but it heads to the north part of the city, where the butcher shop is.

My fingers feel sweaty as I pull my purse onto my shoulder, the nerves kicking into high gear.

Every step I get closer to him, I get more nervous about each detail.

I don't have sexy lingerie, but I can wait for him naked.

I didn't pack all of my makeup yesterday when he brought me back to his place, only my mascara, so that's all I have to work with.

I have to clear my throat to get the knot out of it as

I get closer. I know he's working, and he told me to come to him when I was done, so I am.

Part of me recognizes how... docile I'm being. The only thing that keeps me moving forward and only mildly second-guessing all of this, is how easy Bastian is making it for me. He's not giving me hard glares until I look away. He isn't pretending I don't exist. He isn't ignoring me.

Something changed and I don't know what, but he still makes me feel safe. He always has. I may be crazy in other ways. But I know what I've felt for Sebastian for years has merit. There's something real between us, and that's not a white lie. And I wish one of us would have the courage to say it out loud because deep down I know that neither of us can deny it.

I DON'T KNOW if they'll let me stay here now that my uncle's dead. He died last week and right before my eighteenth birthday. The lawyer said he willed everything to me, but with the debt he left behind, they may have to take the house from me to put into the estate.

And then I'll have no one and nowhere to go.

Those are the thoughts that keep me up tonight even though I know school will come tomorrow. I can't keep skipping class, so I need to sleep, but I can't.

I'm so fucking angry. That's what I feel most guilty

about. I had one person who barely even spoke to me, but he let me stay here, and occasionally it felt like we were family. Uncle Travis was a good man, a trucker his whole life, but he didn't much like other people. A lot of the time, I wondered if that meant me too. Being alone for so long will do that to you.

He came home two weeks ago, and we talked about what was coming after high school. Tears flood my eyes again at the thought and I angrily brush them away.

Even if he wasn't physically here for me, or even if he never showed me much of anything other than a place to stay, I knew without a doubt last week that he loved me.

And now he's gone. It's not fair.

I take in a staggered breath and try to calm down as I cling to my pillow. I've never felt as selfish as I do now, being filled with anger when I should be mourning him.

What's wrong with me?

Just as I think the question, I hear the floorboards creak behind me, toward the open door to the hall.

A shiver runs down my spine as my eyes open wider and then narrow. Swallowing thickly, I know it wasn't just the chill in the air that made the old boards bend in the night. I can hear whoever it is walking closer.

It better be him, *I think bitterly as I reach slowly into the nightstand. My uncle left everything to me, and that means his gun too.*

"You don't need it," *the deep voice calls out from the doorway just as my fingertips brush the cold metal. Slowly shutting the drawer, I let my eyes close and try to calm the adrenaline racing through my body.*

"Why are you here?" I ask him without turning to face him. My chest aches with a pain I can't describe. Sebastian used to come all the time at night when I first moved in here.

"It's been a while," I tell him and hate the nostalgia in my tone.

He's quiet; he always is.

He kissed me, he followed me, and then he left me alone.

"I'm fine," I tell him and then turn in bed, slowly bringing myself up to sit cross-legged under the covers. "As fine as I can be." Years ago, when he'd come, he wouldn't leave until he believed me when I said those words.

And I loved him for it. Truly and deeply, I loved him for it. If it had been anyone else, I'd have been terrified, angry and a mix of everything hateful, but it's not just anyone. It's Sebastian.

Tears cloud my vision of his dark shadowy frame in the doorway.

"You don't look fine."

"Well gee," I say sarcastically, bitterly even as I wipe my eyes. "So kind of you to point out the obvious." It's been years since he's visited me and I'm not the same person I was back then. I've stopped praying for him to come and wishing he'd slip into bed with me and hold me.

I don't want to be held by anyone anymore. *Even as I think it, I know it's not true.*

"Just go," I tell him and then lie down, turning my back to him and pulling the covers up closer to my face so I can use the soft bedding to wipe at my eyes. "You're good at leaving," I add and hate myself for even bothering to speak with him when he merely chuckles. It's a deep low rumble that fills the bedroom and sends a shiver of want across my skin, igniting something I thought was long forgotten. It seems the hate I have for him leaving me, ignoring me day in and day out isn't enough to drown out the desire to be held by him after all.

"Someone told me you might be leaving."

"Who said that?" I barely speak the question. My heart does a stupid pitter-patter at the thought of leaving him. My heart is stupid. I listen as he walks into the bedroom. He stops somewhere far from the bed, but I don't know where and I don't turn to look at him.

"Are you leaving?" he asks me.

"I hope not," I answer him, and the truth of that answer makes me close my eyes tightly. I couldn't wait to get out of here, but I need a place to stay. Everyone needs a home, somewhere they can run to.

"Is it money? Or are you moving somewhere else to be with other family?" he asks me.

"There is no other family," I admit, feeling lonelier by the second.

"So, it's money?"

Time ticks by slowly until I answer him, "Yeah."

He's quiet and doesn't say anything for a long time. So

long, I think maybe he's left me until he says, "It'll be okay. Go to sleep, Chloe Rose."

I REMEMBER THINKING how much I wish I didn't want him to be here as I drifted to sleep, feeling his eyes on me. But I did. I had no one. And of everyone in this place, he was the only one I wanted. So, if that was the way I could have him, I'd take it.

I don't know if he heard me later that night when I woke up and started to cry out of nowhere. I confessed how much I missed him and how lonely I was as I wiped the tears away, still huddled in my spot, gripping the pillow. Or maybe that part was a dream. It's hard to know anymore.

SEBASTIAN

"Well, you only have one more year," I tell Carter.

"I don't have time for it," he answers me as he bounces the old tennis ball against the worn brick of the building.

"You don't have time for school?" I ask him in a tone that's as filled with disbelief as my expression is. "Remind me again, where is it that you make your money?"

Carter's being a dipshit. "You don't need to start working for Romano. You need to graduate, and you can make that extra cash from the schoolyard."

He's a dealer at Crescent Hills High, only pot but he makes some good cash since he's the only one with good shit in this area. The only other dealers are past

Walnut Street and the highway that runs behind it, but those are claimed territories, one of them being Romano's.

"Romano's never going to hire you anyway since you're Irish."

I feel like a prick reminding him that he'll never be trusted, but it's for his own damn good. He should be focused on finishing school and then he can figure out a way to go down south and make some good cash at the fishery on the docks or some other shit. Something better than this.

"You don't get it." His voice is tight and his teeth are clenched. "We have bills."

He throws the ball harder at the wall and catches it after it ricochets with a force that sounds like it hurt. "You forget there's more than one person I have to look after."

It fucking hurts every time he brings it up. To me, he's my kid brother. To him, he's the older brother taking care of his family. A family I'm not a part of.

"It's good money," I remind him. "Both the fishery and the pot. Romano's not going to pay you shit."

I'm still shaking my head when he looks back at me. "Because I'm fucking Irish?"

"Because he doesn't have a need for you." I'm blunt and harsh and my stomach twists. There's no room for him in Romano's territory, but even if there was, I'd lie.

He doesn't have the stomach for this shit. He should be better than me. He *is* better than me. I get paid to fuck up people who owe money to the wrong guys, assholes who think they can steal from establishments who pay for protection. I get paid to be a villain, a thug, and a version of myself I hate. It used to help with the anger; it made me feel like there was a purpose to it all. But that's bullshit. I fucking hate who I am, and I don't want this life for him. I don't want it for anyone.

It's quiet other than the thud of the ball hitting the brick as he considers everything.

"It's just one more year, Carter."

"A lot can change in a year." His voice is muted, low and defeated. I know he wants a change because of his mom, but I can't help him there. I can't keep her from dying. The rubble beneath my feet kicks up as I walk to the cement steps and face the parking lot.

"Is that Chloe?" Carter asks me, and I have to get up to look down the street.

Just the sight of her pulls my lips up into an asymmetric grin. "Yeah, that's her."

"So much for picking her up," he tells me with a glint in his eyes. I check my watch and see she's early, then peek back up at her.

With her jeans hugging her curves, I watch as she walks up the street, not taking my eyes off her.

"Real quick," Carter tries to get my attention, so I

give him a short hum of an answer to let him know I heard him, but I refuse to look away from her as she walks to me.

"Can you come with me to give my dad that money?" His question is enough to break the stare I have on her. He adds, "Tomorrow night?"

"Yeah, of course," I answer him with a shrug like it's no big deal. His mom's bills are adding up, so I'm loaning him some cash to keep them afloat. But the last time I did that, Carter's dad laid into him, thinking he stole it and wanting to know from where.

It's not really a loan, as I never want to be paid back, but Carter insists I call it that. For only being sixteen with not much to be proud of, he's a proud kid.

"How is she doing with everything?" Carter asks to change the subject. I know that's why he did it. "Is she still freaking out?"

My gaze is brought back to her as he asks. Nice timing on his part, as she's just walking up the parking lot.

"She slept at my place last night," I tell him. She slept easily and deep like she hadn't slept in years, waking up with a yawn and a stretch that was so relaxed and at ease. Although the second she saw me, she blushed violently and tried to hide under the covers. "Good morning," were the first words she greeted me with as she covered her mouth and hid under the sheets.

146

Carter's chuckle cuts off any thoughts of sharing particulars. "So that's how you deal with it," he says and nods his head in approval with a wide grin.

If I had that ball in my hands, I'd throw it at him. But damn if the pride in my chest won't go away at him thinking I fucked her worries away.

"Hey." Chloe gives a hello while she's still a good ten feet away, walking through the parking lot and to the back behind the shop where we're standing.

Thump, Carter tosses the ball at the wall, but I don't break my gaze from her. She's already blushing. Her skin is so beautiful like that, with that rosy tinge creeping up her cheeks and growing hotter every second I keep my eyes on her.

"I don't get a hello?" Carter asks jokingly, and for the first time since she's walked up here, her attention goes to him.

"What makes you think I wasn't waiting for you to say hello first?" she asks him, quipping back without missing a beat and with the trace of a friendly smile on her lips. I can see she's a little tense; it's the way she is around people. Tense at first, quiet too, but if she wants, Chloe opens up easily and what's inside is raw and beautiful.

Carter grins back at her as he says, "Hello." He pronounces the word carefully, enunciating each syllable and it makes her laugh although that shyness is still there.

"Are you working here too?" she asks him and the hair raise on the back of my neck. Everyone here works for Romano, but Carter needs something better than this. I keep my thoughts to myself and wait for him to reply.

"Still in school," he answers and she's quick to add, "I always forget you're younger than us."

It's odd how she says it. Like she knows him or maybe she's just paired us together like other people have.

"Were your ears burning?" Carter asks her with his brow raised. "We were just talking about you."

Chloe hums a small laugh with her lips closed tight although she can't hide her smile. "I hope good things," she adds after a moment of the two of us staring at her and waiting for her reply.

"Mostly," Carter jokes with her, but I can tell he makes her nervous by the way her smile slips.

"Yeah," she says honestly. "I kind of figured you might be..." her voice trails off and she offers me a small smile although I can see how nervous she is. She picks at the hem of her shirt while she talks. "I might have been talking about you too," she tells me, biting down on her lip after and looking me up and down.

"Is that right?" I ask her and she's quick to shake her head. "No, I'm just playing."

Carter barks out a laugh while I stand there looking like an asshole.

"I didn't give you anything good to talk about?" I joke with her, but she just clears her throat, slowly letting those walls come back up.

She didn't talk about me because she has no one to talk to. I feel like a prick when the realization hits me.

"I'll make that up to you tonight then," I add before she has to say anything. Her cheeks must be on fire to be that red.

I let my hand travel to the small of her back to lead her away and I nod a goodbye to Carter. He's waiting for the bus to go to the hospital, but it'll be here in minutes. It's almost 5:15.

"See you later, Carter," Chloe says sweetly, giving him a small wave as I walk her to my car.

I open the door for her, but before she can slip in, I wrap my hand around her hip and bring her closer to me. I have one hand on the door, with the other on her hip and her stance mirrors mine. It's as if she's waiting for what my next move will be, so she can determine hers.

Her lips are parted and her eyes dart between my gaze and where Carter's standing behind me.

All I wanted was to give her a small kiss. So, I do, just a short one on her lips. Pressing my mouth to hers and making sure to run the tip of my nose over hers. The cops already know; people are already talking. Might as well give them a show.

That shy smile I love plays on her lips and she can barely look me in the eyes.

"You nervous?" I whisper against her cheek before pulling away. Her wide eyes stay on mine as she settles into the seat and answers honestly in a single breath, "Yeah."

CHLOE

$\mathcal{M}$y heart's being stupid. It keeps fluttering and flipping all sorts of ways like it's trying to escape or run away. I try to swallow again, but I can't. Instead, I snuggle closer to Sebastian on the sofa, although every inch of his side is covered with mine right now.

It's just sex.

I keep reminding myself. Every time the nerves work their way up from my heart to my brain, I have to remind myself. It's just sex.

Not just that, but every part of me feels like it was supposed to be this way. Like Sebastian was meant to have me. Even the little bits of me hidden away in the pages of my books, all the way down to the marrow in my bones; it was supposed to happen like this.

I haven't told him, although I almost did earlier. We

were sitting on the sofa, but not cuddling like this, sitting cross-legged, and eating Chinese food from the cartons. He's been good at keeping the conversation going and giving me those cocky smiles. I think he's drawing it out on purpose.

First dinner and now a movie, although it's almost over.

And thus, my heart is doing that stupid thing knowing the movie will be over soon. I swallow it all down as best I can and nestle my head into Sebastian's chest.

"You comfortable?" he asks me although it sounds like he's picking on me. I only hum a response.

"You can't go to sleep," he tells me, and instantly my eyelids fall shut just to fuck with him. He shrugs his shoulder and I give him a look.

"Stop moving," I complain in as flirtatious of a voice as I can and feel pride rise when he rewards me with that charming smile of his that drives me wild.

He smells like fresh woods, the kind you want to get lost in; his body is hard and dominating. Every piece of him chiseled like Adonis. I splay my hand on his chest and revel in the fact that he's letting me.

Back in school, I thought that he was avoiding me because he was older. At least at first. Then when I realized who he was and why everyone else avoided him, I wondered how a boy like him could be interested in a girl like me. The more he avoided me, the stupider I felt.

When the only piece of reality you crave is revealed to be all in your head, it does something awful to you.

"I like you coming to me after work, but I could have picked you up." Sebastian starts up a conversation as the credits to the comedy scroll on the screen. If someone asked me to repeat a line from what we just watched, I'd come up with nothing. All I'm thinking about is how Sebastian is going to fuck me.

I've masturbated but I don't know if I have a hymen or not. I've used a few toys I've read about in books although I don't often feel the need to do that. Not unless I read a steamier romance. Or one where the hero reminds me of Sebastian.

"I wanted to leave work early. It was a short walk." I answer him with a shrug and try to keep my train of thought on the fact that he hasn't made a move yet. He hasn't done anything other than to put his arm around my shoulder and pull me to close to him under the covers on the sofa.

"You sure like to walk everywhere," he remarks like he doesn't like it.

"I don't mind it." It's one of the things that took me a long time to do alone. I don't know if it's because I was old enough to understand what happened to my mother, or if I was always afraid of walking alone, but learning to accept the fear and proving it wrong is one way to cope. "Sometimes it's nice," I add, swallowing down the memories that beg to ruin this moment.

Sebastian shifts on the sofa and it dips, making me fall slightly.

"You ready for bed?" he asks me, pulling me back up by my waist and shifting me into his lap. His warm breath tickles my shoulder as he kisses me for the first time since we came back to his place. Right on the crook of my neck, sending shivers down my body and hardening my nipples.

My body feels alive with need. Every nerve ending is waiting to go off and sitting on an edge that feels so close.

With both of my eyes closed, I hum a response. "I was wondering what was taking you so long," I tell him as he stands, leaving me with the chill of his immediate absence and forcing me to open my eyes.

He offers me a hand and I take it to stand but he only smirks at me, not giving me any words in the least.

Cue my stupid heart.

It's just sex.

That ball of nerves threatens to suffocate me as I walk in time with Sebastian to the bedroom. He doesn't waste any time stripping down to nothing. So, I follow suit. First my shirt and then my pants, but by the time I'm left in my bra and underwear, he's already naked and stroking his erection.

Oh, my God.

My pussy heats and clenches around nothing. Fire blazes inside of me. I can't take my stare away from him as he strokes himself.

He's cocky as he asks me, "Need a hand?"

A voice inside of me begs me to tell him I haven't done this before, but instead, I meet his gaze steadily and unhook my bra, letting it fall carelessly to the floor. Then I easily step out of my thong, even though I know he's let his own gaze wander to my body.

He doesn't say anything. No comment on my body at all as I walk to the bed and get under the covers. It's dark in his bedroom, but there's enough light enough to see. There's hardly any light from the windows with the curtains drawn even though there are streetlights close by. And he left the hall light on, which he didn't do yesterday, so that had to be on purpose. So, he could see.

Adrenaline races through my veins as the bed groans with his weight and dips.

Still, I feel like he can see everything. Even as I'm hiding under the covers.

"No covers," he says with a playfulness I wasn't expecting. "I get to have you my way tonight, Chloe Rose," he teases me.

"I'm cold." The excuse slips easily from my lips as my heart pounds furiously in my chest.

His lips find mine in a slow, languid kiss. His hot tongue dips into my mouth as he pulls back the covers.

Suddenly, I actually am cold. In every place, he isn't touching me, and I feel like I'll freeze to death if his hands don't find every inch of my body right this second.

He breaks the kiss, towering over me and climbing on top of me to tell me, "I'll warm you up." I expect another kiss, but his lips fall to the dip below my collar. One kiss there, then one an inch below. I can't breathe.

Goosebumps flow down my arms and the heat burrows itself in the pit of my stomach.

"I'm hot," I moan out into the air and then my eyes open wide, realizing what I said. Sebastian could tease me, taunt me for being hot and cold, but all he does is kiss lower and lower, fueling the fire that licks over my body.

By the time his stubble is tickling my inner thighs, my hands are on his shoulders, my blunt nails digging into his skin. I'm at war with myself, not knowing if I want to push him down that last inch or push him away for fear of being inadequate.

A single languid lick from my entrance to my clit has my back bowing.

Sebastian chuckles and the vibrations nearly send me over. My cheeks are hot with embarrassment, but the threat of pushing me over so soon is looming larger and more aggressively than anything else I could feel.

His tongue flicks my clit and again I buck my hips, but his hands are already there, pushing me down and keeping me in place. Panting, I struggle to breathe and to know where to put my hands. So, I grab the sheets and fist them as he sucks my clit and massages it with his tongue.

My toes curl and a strangled sound is forced from me. With my eyes closed, I don't see him, but I feel all of him. He shoves his fingers inside of me and a pool of desire ignites in my core when he does it, forcing my back to arch and sending waves of heat through my body that feel uncontained.

With his mouth on my clit and his fingers inside me, I scream out his name from the pleasure that rolls through me. I push myself into his face shamelessly.

He finger fucks me brutally and doesn't let up on either ministration until I'm biting down on my lip hard enough to hurt and cumming on his hand.

The paralyzing pleasure rolls through me in waves like a vengeful tide, taking from me ruthlessly. I can't breathe or even move as he leaves kisses along my curves and guides the head of his dick to my entrance.

The battering ram in my chest is at it again and I force my head to turn, to look him in the eyes and nearly tell him.

But his eyes are filled with shades of blue so bright, so filled with the frenzy of passion, that even if I could stop him at this moment, I wouldn't. I won't take this from him. He was meant to have me. And this is how he wanted me.

"I want to feel you," he says, and his plea is a deep rumble of desire. He nudges the tip of his nose against mine. "No condom?" he asks.

No words come to me, so I simply nod my head and kiss him, eager to feel him too.

His large body is hot against mine and I shut my eyes as I'm inundated with emotion as he hovers over me, but without my eyes on him, he growls. It sounds like a growl. Deep and low in his chest, primal and threatening.

My eyes whip back to him and he crashes his lips to mine. With a gasp, I open for him and he uses that moment to spread my legs wider, nestling his hips between my legs and pushing himself inside of me just slightly.

I'm overwhelmed. Unable to come back from the high of my pleasure, from the high of knowing Sebastian wants me, and from the all-consuming kiss that he devours me with, I'm completely at his mercy.

I brace myself, ready for him to shove himself inside of me in one swift stroke. For him to tear through me and take me how I've always wanted him to, but as his heart slams against his chest and in tandem with mine, he pulls away from our kiss and nudges the tip of his nose against mine once again. My lashes flutter open and I stare into his gaze as he slowly pushes himself into me.

His lips are parted, and they widen just slightly as he lets out a deep breath and moves deeper inside of me.

I can't help that my lips part as well, that they form an O as he stretches me and the sharp pain of it mixes with the sweet, lingering pleasure. As he rocks out of me and then back in, he mutters with his eyes closed, "You're so tight," and I don't know what to say.

I should tell him, but I don't. I don't want to change anything.

"Take me," I beg him in a whispered plea and reach up to grab his shoulders while wrapping my legs around his hips.

I wasn't prepared for him to slam inside of me. For him to lower his lips to the crook of my neck as he fills me completely and stretches me beyond what I can handle. He groans a deep masculine sound of satisfaction as he tears through me, breathing me in and taking my virginity in a single movement. The pain makes me close my eyes tightly, it makes me tense and dig my heels into his ass. I feel hot and full, and it's too much. It hurts. Fuck, it hurts. It's more than I can handle.

But with my teeth clenched and no words spoken, Sebastian moves out of me slowly, giving me slight relief. It only lasts for a split second before he savagely slams back into me. My eyes close tight and I bite down on my lip to keep from screaming.

Again, and again, he thrusts, each time picking up his pace and each time the pain mixes with pleasure.

Each time I think it's too much, but every time he pulls away, no matter how briefly, it feels like a loss. I want this, I want him. I want more.

The bliss that thrills every nerve ending is caught in a vise. I can't control how my body begs for more, but it simultaneously wants to push him away.

It hurts.

It fucking hurts.

But it feels so good, it feels like everything I've ever wanted.

As he picks up his pace, my head thrashes, but Sebastian's hands stay on my hips, pushing me down and keeping me right where he wants me. His lips roam my body, sending kisses down my neck and shoulder, over my collarbone and everywhere. It feels like he's everywhere. And it's almost too much— almost, but it's not. I know it's not because my body wants to focus on how viciously he's fucking me.

My body focuses on the intense pain and equally intense pleasure.

Tears leak from the corner of my eyes, and I struggle to breathe, but somehow, I cry out his name. "Bastian." It's a single strangled breath. It's not from the pain, not all of it anyway. It's from everything. I'm losing myself to him and it's everything. I wish I could stop the well of emotion pouring up from me, but with every thrust, every sound, every touch from him... I can't stop it.

My nails rake down his back as he shoves himself deep inside of me, past the brink of pain and toward something blinding, numbing yet igniting. My head falls back limply as the pleasure rips through me, tearing every bit of me apart into a million pieces.

And then he stops, and the world is motionless with the orgasm still racing through me.

"Chlo?" Sebastian's voice is full of worry as the rough pad of his thumb wipes at the tears still falling down my face.

"Don't stop," I beg him but even my voice sounds pained, and he pulls himself out of me.

"Fuck, are you okay?" he asks me and reaches across me to the nightstand, turning on the bright light. I can only close my eyes as the pleasure still rages through me. The dull pain turns to a vibrant ache as I try to close my legs and involuntarily let out a pained moan as I curl over on my side.

"No, fuck," Sebastian's voice, full of worry and regret sends embarrassment and shame through me, and the tears come on harder and I can't stop them. My body is confused and the emotions inside of me are welling up and I can't stop them.

"I'm fine," I barely manage to say as I wipe at the embarrassing tears.

"Don't lie to me, what did I do?" He sounds angry as he tries to push my legs apart. "Fuck," is the last word he says before climbing off the bed and running to the bathroom. As my eyes adjust to the light, I peer down my body to see bright red staining the sheets. Both of my hands cover my face with the regret, and dread overwhelms me to the point where I wish I could disappear.

"I'm sorry." I hear Sebastian before I see him, but even as I register his words, he's already on the bed. He rubs a damp, warm washcloth soothingly on my inner thigh to clean me up.

The shock from the concern on his expression and how carefully he's cleaning me without worrying about the sheets keeps me from being able to speak.

He kisses my outer thigh with his eyes still open, gives me another kiss and gets closer. "I'm sorry," he whispers against my skin. "I knew you were tight, but fuck... I didn't mean to hurt you." I can't stand the look in his eyes like this was his fault. Like he has anything to be sorry for at all.

"I'm a virgin." The words leave an awful feeling in my throat as they come up like I'm suffocating. "I was... before... I should have told you," I whisper with my eyes closed.

And there's nothing but silence. He doesn't move or

speak for what feels like forever. But finally, he asks, "Does it hurt?" I shake my head no as quickly as I can, refusing to cry anymore.

"You're crying, Chlo, please don't lie to me. I'll never forgive myself."

"Please, just pretend I'm not," I try to plead with him, my eyes still closed tightly and my hands reaching up to cover my face.

"Fuck that," he tells me, grabbing my hands and pulling them away. "Tell me the truth," his sternly spoken words force my eyes open. Through the haze of tears, I stare into his demanding gaze. "Did I hurt you?"

I shake my head, searching for the words to explain. "It's a mix, but the more you..." I have to pause and swallow before continuing, "the more you're inside of me, the better..." I struggle to calm myself and my racing heart, which doesn't seem so stupid now for wanting to escape earlier. If I could vanish now, I would.

His hand cups my jaw, his thumb running along my bottom lip before he asks me, "Would you tell me to stop if it was too much?" Before he can even finish his question, I'm shaking my head.

"I need you to," he demands. His voice is laced with concern plus a plea I don't expect. "I need you to tell me." His eyes search mine, glancing over my face as he brushes the tears away. With him maneuvering himself back to where he was, my body calms and the heat lingers in my core.

"I want you," I beg him. "Please, I need this to be--"

"I want you too." His words calm every bit of anxiety and I reach up to kiss him, but it's shortened as he pulls away.

"You can have me," he whispers before giving me a chaste kiss I try to deepen, "but you need to tell me if it hurts too much." He says the last part with his eyes closed and then opens them, piercing me with his gaze. "Don't do that again," he warns me. "Don't let me hurt you."

His words are so full of certainty and a darkness I can't deny, so I speak immediately. "I won't. "I'm sorry," I quickly add and feel the weight of regret bury the embarrassment.

"I'm afraid if you never tell me, I'll never know." His confession makes me repeat myself, "I'm sorry."

"Look at me, Chlo," he says then grabs my chin between his thumb and forefinger. Without hesitating he kisses me once, then again and a third time, silencing the doubt and regret. A kiss from Sebastian Black soothes everything. He is the healing balm to my soul. As long as he kisses me, as long as he wants my lips to brush against his, I'm safe and cherished in a way I can't describe. Even if it's all in my head, it's all I need.

With his eyes closed, his forehead resting against

mine, he whispers between us, "If you don't tell me, I will hurt you. I know I will. I know it. And I don't want to."

I nudge him with my nose to get him to look at me. "It hurt, but it was going too regardless," I tell him and try to make him understand. "I thought I could hide the pain and when I couldn't, it didn't matter anyway because it felt... like everything." I cling to his shoulders and make him look me in the eyes. "I promise you, I want this." I breathe once, just once, waiting for him to say anything. "I want you and I want you to have me how you want."

"We have time for me to... to," he swallows thickly, "Chlo, I wanted to fucking destroy you." His words make me blush furiously. I watch the way he swallows, mesmerized by his confession as he adds, "I wanted to make sure you still felt me tomorrow, so whoever had gotten to you before me, didn't stand a chance at being remembered as a good lay."

"It's okay," I say but can barely get the words out. The idea of still feeling him inside of me tomorrow and what his intentions were does nothing but fill me with lust and make me wish I hadn't cried. I wish I could have hidden the pain like I've read about before. "You can have me, however--"

"Knock it off, Chlo," Sebastian reprimands, but he says it with a smile that calms my nerves. "I want you to remember this for other reasons. Now that I know..."

I'm hot all over and still trying to gain control of my body and my emotions when he tells me, "Don't hide this shit from me, Chloe Rose. I'll find out." His command comes out more teasing than anything else as he nudges his nose against mine. He reaches between his legs, his arm brushing my clit as he does, and it makes my head fall back against the pillow.

"I'll tell you everything," I promise him with the sweet feeling of pleasure building. He's stroking himself and moving back to where he was, but every small movement brushes against me too, burning hotter than before.

"Then tell me you want me."

The rhythm of my heart skips a beat. "I want you, Sebastian."

It races as he tells me, "Spread your legs for me." I obey him instantly. With him guiding himself back inside of me, I try to hide the wince from the lingering, stinging pain, but he sees. "I'll make it feel good." His words are soothing as he pushes himself inside of me and captures my scream with his kiss.

He rocks his hips steadily, each time brushing his pubic bone to my clit and he never takes his lips from mine. So long as I can kiss him back, he keeps his pace and massages his tongue along mine in swift strokes. A warmth floods through me as the pain morphs into divine pleasure.

I gasp for breath the second he parts his lips from mine, but then immediately he seeks them again. My eyes are closed and every touch of is his gentle, save the ruthless way he fucks me.

"Harder," I beg him while gasping for air, but instead of harder, he moves his hand between us and pushes his thumb to my clit.

Fireworks go off along my skin and deep in the pit of my stomach and lower.

With every thrust from him, I gasp. The sounds of our breathing, of him fucking me and the bed protesting, only fuel me to want more. I don't dare rip my eyes from his gaze as I cum, feeling him cum with me. I can feel everything, the way he pulses and puts more pressure against my walls, the way he fills me.

And then when he pulls away, I feel everything. Every sensation and tingling need to curl onto my side and recover from what he's done to me. My body's trembling, literally shaking.

I hear him go to the bathroom, but I can't open my eyes to see him. It feels like he's still there. I'm swollen and the ache is still raw.

But so is this feeling that takes over every inch of me. The rolling tide of pleasure that refuses to leave.

When he comes back to the bed, I want to ask him if it's always like that, but I don't.

Instead, I ask him if he wants me to take off the sheets, in a voice still breathless, but he shushes me, getting in behind me and scooting me to the other side of the bed. Even with fatigue weighing me down and the overwhelming sensation of pleasure still racing through me, I want to do something for him, anything.

Theres's a crushing need to make things right with him, to show him that it's okay and even better than okay. And that I'm sorry. I feel so fucking sorry.

But he hushes me again and plants a kiss on the side of my jaw, wrapping his heavy arm around me and pulling me close.

"Thank you," I whisper although I feel foolish doing it. Sebastian doesn't say anything; he just holds me tighter. I don't know if I've ruined everything and part of me starts to wonder if I have. It was intense and emotional and I'm still riding the high, but the nagging feeling that I'm alone, and that I destroyed whatever we had creeps into my thoughts.

"How did that feel, Chloe Rose?" The deep rumble of his chest accompanies his question.

It felt like he owned me. Body and soul.

"You can do that to me whenever you want," I answer him with sweet sorrow mixing in my chest. I don't know what tomorrow will bring, but tonight, I'll have forever.

He arranges me so I'm nestled perfectly against his chest on my side, his hand splayed on my belly as he kisses my hair and then my shoulder. Nothing but warmth and comfort flow through me. I've never felt so loved. Never in my life have I felt like this. So wholly wanted and cherished. It's the way he's brutal, but gentle just the same. I want to believe it's because of me, because of us. That it isn't like this with other girls. That he isn't treating me differently because he found out I'm a virgin. And although the doubt and worry are there, tonight it feels real.

I swear I hear him whisper, "I love you, Chloe Rose," as my eyes become heavier. He whispered it at the back of my neck. But as quickly as I thought I heard the words, I start to think I imagined it. It's something I've always wanted to hear from him, and I need to hear it now. I desperately need to hear it.

I don't know if it's a dream, maybe one I once had long ago and wish to remember, or if it's real. But as I feel sleep pull me under, I hold on to those words. Deep down inside of my soul, I know they'll keep me safe.

I only wish I had the strength to say them to him.

SEBASTIAN

How could I not have known?

I can't get the nagging thought to go the fuck away. I was so eager to have Chloe, to ruin her, to make sure she'd remember me forever, that I didn't stop to consider the possibility I'd be her first.

If I had known, I would have done it differently. She'd have a better memory of her first time.

I should have fucking known.

Drew dated her for a month when I was away, up north with Romano. He told me he was lying about the rumors of her sucking him off behind the school, but at the time, I wasn't sure if he was telling me the truth or not because I was slamming his face into the cement. I thought he took her first. The day I heard what he was telling other people, I thought he'd taken her V-card.

Her only other boyfriend was Jared Santack.

They went to semi formals together and I saw him kiss her. I know they went home together that night. It was the night I came home from my first stint in jail. I remember thinking for a split second how she deserved someone like Jared, then I planned how I'd fuck up his car the next day, just because he needed to have something of his broken too.

"What the hell is wrong with you?" Carter asks me from across the dining room.

My gaze shifts to him and I try to fix the pissed off look I know is on my face, but I can't. Last night fucked me up in a way I can't explain. I run my hand down my face and try to shrug it all off. The chair legs scratch on the floor as I get up from the table and go to the window. Carter's family's house is on the outskirts of the city and backs up to the woods. It's dark and there's not much to look at out there, but I stare outside anyway, trying to get my shit together.

My knuckles rap on the worn-out buffet table in front of the window as he asks me, "She getting to you?"

Is Chloe Rose getting to me?

She's *always* gotten to me.

I don't answer him, instead, I try to make up a lie, but it doesn't occur to me that the lie is a truth until the words are spoken. "Being here just reminds me of family," I tell him. My spine stiffens and a chill runs through me.

"Shit, man," Carter tells me, "I'm sorry." As if it's his fault. As if he has anything at all to be sorry about.

I shake it off, hating that tonight of all nights I'm making this about me. That I can't focus and be there for my only friend.

"How did the treatment go?" I ask him. And the look on his face instantly changes. The sympathy morphs into anguish.

He doesn't say anything, although he tries. Instead, he looks me in the eyes and shakes his head.

My heart drops down to the pit of my stomach. "Fuck." It's all I can give him and then we're both looking out the window.

"Tell me something good."

His request catches me off guard and I consider him for a moment.

Something good. It takes me longer than it should to think of something. All thoughts lead back to Chloe Rose.

"I fucked Chlo last night," I tell him. "I was her first."

"Shit, really?" he asks. "She's twenty?" I nod, waiting for him to say something else. For him to understand what it meant to me. But I don't think he will. No one will. They don't get it. I don't even understand it.

Ever since I laid eyes on her, she was mine. It didn't matter that I didn't want anyone, because I didn't have a choice. She was mine. Fate picked her for me, and vice versa. Last night was meant to happen. I know it.

The sound of the door opening distracts us both, drawing our attention to the front door we can't see.

Carter grabs the edge of the buffet tighter at the sound of his dad calling out for him. "Back here," he replies and steels himself, staring straight ahead and trying to relax his posture.

I fucking hate it. I hate how he's scared of his own father. He tells me it's the way it is and that it's no different from how his father was raised, but that doesn't make it right.

I expect his father to be drunk and angry, like the last few times I've seen him. He pissed himself the one night he was so hammered, we had to drag him home.

His steps get louder and then the old man is right in front of us, his hands slipping into his pockets as he leans against the doorway. "You two eat already?" he asks us and gives me a short nod before pulling out a smoke.

He lights up as we answer him. I can feel the aggression rolling off of me, my expression getting tighter, but I know that's no good for Carter. He doesn't want a war, he just wants to do what's right by his mom.

Mr. Cross walks to the dining room table, sifting through the bills and puffing on his cigarette.

"How is she?" Carter asks him, and I glance between the two of them. His father's expression falters for a split second before he changes it to something else, something stronger than the weak man who's withering away just as his wife is.

He nods at Carter and tells him, "She had a good day." With his lips pressed in a thin line, he tells us he's going to bed. Carter told me the days he doesn't drink are different, but I haven't seen him like this in a long time. A long damn time. It's been two years of hell, with my hate growing for this man, but seeing him sober is different.

Carter nudges me as his father starts to walk away and I reach in my back pocket for the cash. "Mr. Cross," I call out to him and take the three steps forward to pass him the bundle. "I just wanted to help out if you'll take it," I offer. "I won it on a bet and I don't need it."

"I wish I had the decency not to," he answers me. "This isn't charity."

"Call it a loan then," I answer him quickly as he tries to give it back. Taking a step away from him, I tell him, "I don't care either way." He nods his head in agreement, but the old man's eyes turn paler and glossy.

It's quiet for a long time as I watch the man do his best not to break down in front of me, tapping the wad of cash against his palm.

"I don't know how to tell your brothers." He talks to Carter without looking at me, staring down at the cash before slapping it down on the dining room table. The strength he had diminishes, and his face crumples with hopelessness.

"She's not going to be here for much longer," he starts to cry and it fucking hurts watching a grown man lose it. "I can't lose your mother." He covers his face with one hand, his other bracing him on the table to keep himself upright.

"They know, Dad," Carter tells him, although he doesn't go to his dad, he doesn't try to comfort him. He stands strong and his father only seems to respect the decision as he rights himself, brushing away the tears and sniffling hard to be done with it.

"They don't know," he says in a single breath, his face going stony. "They can't know until it happens. Nothing can prepare you for it."

Carter looks down and stares at his mud-covered boots; I know he wants to object.

His father's right though. Even knowing the end is coming can't help. Nothing can prepare you for the type of destruction death brings.

"We'll be all right," his father sniffs and grabs Carter's shoulder, squeezing it and waiting for Carter to look him in the eye. "All boys," his father says and huffs a humorless laugh although a faint smile is on his lips. He looks at me as he asks, "Can you believe that?"

I offer him a weak laugh, feeling awkward and out of place.

"Their mother wanted a little girl and instead I gave her five sons. All Irish; the Irish boys have to be tough." He nods his head as he talks to neither of us in particular. "The men have to be tough," he repeats and then gives his son's shoulder one more squeeze.

"Carter will do good," he says and then sniffles again, giving me a glance before walking toward the worn doorway. "Carter will take care of them," he says softly.

"You're talking like you're already dead," Carter comments. "You're still here." The tension between them changes to something else, and for the first time, I see why Carter doesn't blame his father. He would never go against his father. It's the fear of losing him that keeps him loyal. Between the alcohol and his hopelessness, he's already close to losing him.

"I won't live much longer after she goes. That's how it works." His father doesn't say anything else in the awkward silence that follows and neither does Carter.

It's only when the stairs creak with the weight of his father going to bed, that Carter says anything.

"He's a different man when he isn't drinking. You see it, right?" Carter asks me, his voice more hopeful than I thought it'd be. "He's not all bad."

I can only nod, not wanting to fight with Carter. Carter's told me his father treats him differently from Daniel, who's the second oldest. He's told me some days he doesn't even know if his father loves him. I can't forgive a man for treating his son like that. I won't.

"Thanks for the loan, man," he tells me, even though I'm aware he doesn't like that he had to take it.

"Yeah, no problem. It's nothing," I say and try to brush it off like it doesn't matter. "I have to go home to Chlo."

"Look at you," Carter jokes and I can feel the tension leave him, grateful to move on to a different subject. "Don't fuck it up."

I almost joke back and tell him that I know I'm going to ruin it somehow. But it's too close to the truth and I don't want to speak life into the words.

It wasn't supposed to be this way in my head, not like this.

"She has no one," I tell Carter, just wanting him to understand her the way I do. "The worst thing I can imagine is having no one." It's only when the words are spoken that I realize how alone I've really been. I wait for Carter to say something, but his mind is elsewhere.

Maybe there is something worse though. Like having someone, but knowing you're bound to lose them.

CHLOE

$\mathcal{I}$t's weird being alone in this place without Sebastian. I'm surprised he let me stay here at all. I'd planned on sneaking out in the morning and being weird on my own rather than weird with him.

The biggest fucking lie I've ever told myself is that this is just sex. Last night was more than sex for me.

I woke up a few hours after I'd passed out, and I couldn't get back to sleep. I was wide awake and so very aware of everything that happened. With his arm still around me, I wanted so badly to stay in that moment. The moment where it felt like he still wanted me.

I knew it would hurt down there, and at 4 a.m. every tiny shift in my body seemed to be connected to the ache between my legs. It still hurts now in the evening after. I knew it would. But I didn't expect the emotional change, the emotional pain that comes with it.

Not able to sleep, and knowing I'd made a fool of myself, I thought I'd sneak out, leave him a note, and let him decide if he still wanted me. If I was worth still being around or with, or whatever it is that we have going on. I wanted to make it easy for him because I knew what I was doing, and it wasn't fair to him not to tell him.

That was the conclusion I came to at four in the morning as I breathed in his masculine scent one last time and felt the warmth of his hard chest at my back. I closed my eyes and savored that moment, memorizing it, just in case it would be the only moment I had like that with him. Of all the things that have happened between us, that's the one I wanted to hold on to.

Where he took from me what he needed, and I took from him what I needed.

With a deep and slow breath, I carefully crawled out of bed, taking my time and being as quiet and gentle as I could so I wouldn't wake him. It wasn't until my first foot hit the floor that I winced and seethed. It hurt more than I realized.

He woke up instantly, reaching behind him to turn on the lamp. He's so fucking beautiful. It's an odd word for a man, but it's true. With sleep still in his eyes and his stubble longer than usual, he looked groggy but sexy as fuck. Maybe it's the way the light hit him, or maybe it's the hormones and lack of sleep, but I've never been more attracted to a man before. I don't think I ever will be either.

"You all right?" His voice was laced with sleep and accompanied by the bed groaning as he sat up.

"Lie back down, I'm fine," I whispered as if he was being ridiculous, although my heart pounded knowing I was trying to sneak out and failed.

I thought it through right then. He'd turn out the light and lie down, I'd go to the bathroom to clean up. After a while, when I thought he'd fallen asleep again, I'd sneak out and let him text me. I didn't want to risk taking the time to leave a note and making it more awkward than it already was if he caught me.

I could walk to my house from here and at this time of day, no one would be up. There would be no one to bother me on the short walk home.

"You aren't sneaking out, right?" Bastian questioned. "'Cause I want to wake up with you in the morning." He said it so definitively, so sincerely.

If there was ever a moment where I knew I was his completely, it was then.

And that was over twelve hours ago.

Now I'm alone in his house wondering what to do with myself, other than snoop through his shit. Which has been a rather disappointing endeavor.

My phone pings as I close the last drawer in his

dresser, finding nothing but a pair of his pajama pants. They're flannel and smell like him, so I slip them on and with my baggy t-shirt, I couldn't be more comfortable.

Sprawled out on his bed, I check my texts and bust out laughing. I'd texted Angie, *Sex is better than masturbation.*

And she finally responded. *Tell me who, you whore!*

I feel the blush rise to my cheeks, but the butterflies in my chest and belly are more prominent.

I consider telling her, but I'm not ready to share him, so instead, I tell her it has to wait till Monday. I assume the slew of texts afterward are from her, but I lie on the bed, staring up at his ceiling and wondering about how Bastian got to be the way that he is rather than answering them.

Every thought that comes only makes my heart hurt more for him.

The texts don't stop coming and as I remember every detail I know about Bastian and the way he was in high school, they annoy me more and more.

Grabbing my phone off the bed where I tossed it, I'm ready to silence it until I see the most recent text.

Did you hear about Mr. Adler? They found him dead.

My blood runs cold and I swear I feel it all drain from my face. Angie's still messaging me and threatening to do all sorts of stupid shit if I don't confide in her right this second. But I couldn't give two shits about her right now. Mr. Adler was next on the list. I feel fucking sick.

The message is from an unknown number. My fingers shake as I text the person back with the obvious question. *Who is this?*

Breathe, just breathe. I have to keep myself calm even as I start to shake from the adrenaline coursing through me. The fourth person on the list. Right in a row. One. Two. Three. Four. All found dead.

My phone pings and I look down to see a new text from the unknown number. All it reads is: *That doesn't answer my question.*

I can't stop trembling as I stare down at my phone.

Who else would text me? No one. No one else. The only other person who has my number is Marc because I had to give it to him.

I didn't mean to frighten you.

Another message comes through and my heart beats faster. The front door is locked, I know it is, but still, I climb out of bed and check it. It's hard to even swallow with my heart in my fucking throat.

Who is this? I text back and then add, *I'm not frightened. It's fine, I just hadn't heard that Mr. Adler had died.*

I ALMOST WRITE MORE. All lies though. Lies meant to deceive. Something to make it feel casual, normal even. Something that would prove I'm not terrified. But all that's running through my mind is that the person on the other end is a killer. The killer the cops have been looking for and failing to find.

I repeat over and over that I'm not crazy, I'm not paranoid. I remind myself what Sebastian said, that I'm scared and looking for answers. Which I am. Four in a row. It's a fucking hit list.

"Fuck," I grip my hair and clench my teeth before calling Sebastian. My throat's tight as I stand in the middle of the living room, vaguely aware that I'm on the brink of a panic attack.

I'm not crazy. I'm not crazy.

I don't know what to think. Other than someone has a copy of that list, or made the same list, but how?

Voicemail. It goes to voicemail. An hour ago, I felt untouchable here; now I feel like I'm in a cage, unable to go anywhere and so easily seen by anyone who could be watching.

Please call me. I text Sebastian as another text comes through.

I shouldn't have texted you.

Who is this? I ask again, but no reply comes. Not then and not thirty minutes later when I'm huddled in a ball on the sofa, wondering if calling the cops is even an option. There's no news at all that Jeff Adler was found dead. Not on the news online and not a hint of it on any social media.

Is he even dead? And if he is, and the person who texted me knew, but no one else...

The number is still silent an hour later when I leave a voicemail on Sebastian's phone. I wish it wasn't real. I wish I could blink and the messages would be gone. I would rather know I truly am crazy than to be living this nightmare. I don't mention any of it in the voicemail to Sebastian, I just beg him to please come back or return my call. The second I hang up, I lose it.

It's a slow spiral of a breakdown, and maybe that's what the person wanted.

I text the unknown number again and beg them to tell me who they are. And I get nothing. For hours, I have nothing but my own fear and a random text that was designed to inflict it.

Someone wanted to hurt me.

There's only one person I think of over and over again who could be behind this and it proves I'm insane.

It can't be my mother, but when I dig through my purse and find the list, a list no one else knows about, I can't think of anything other than her and the nightmares.

My mother is dead. *It's not her*, I tell myself over and over, resting my cheek against the flannel fabric on my knees and rocking back and forth. It takes everything in me to calm myself down, telling myself that I'm safe here with Sebastian. Whoever it was is an asshole.

Someone who overheard me at the butcher shop maybe. Someone playing a cruel trick on me.

Whoever it is can go fuck themselves.

The anger and hopeful explanation are all that keeps me together. Just barely. I'm holding on by a thread and watching the clock tick by, wondering where Sebastian is and why he hasn't messaged me back.

For hours.

SEBASTIAN

"*W*here were you?" Chlo asks before the front door is even closed. Her voice is filled with accusations that make my body freeze.

Her eyes are bloodshot as she peeks up at me above her knees on the sofa. It's not too late yet. Past dinnertime, but it's not so late that she should be coming at me like this. Unless she knew something.

What the fuck happened? It's all I can think. My movements are slow as I toss the keys on the table and kick off my boots, taking her in as she watches me. My heart's hammering and I'm fucking confused. This isn't my Chloe.

"I was with Carter, they don't get good reception out there," I tell her and hope she accepts it as the truth. "What's wrong?" She can't be mad that I left her alone

186

all day. There's no fucking way that's it when I know for a fact she was going to leave me last night.

"Someone texted me," she says in a quick breath and then closes her eyes to swallow. "I'm being stupid," she says while shaking her head, her eyes closed tightly.

"What'd they say?" I ask her, trying to hide the adrenaline and rage that mixes in a deadly concoction. I walk carefully to her, watching as she rubs her eyes. Sitting close to her and pulling her into me, I try to calm her down so she'll just talk to me. And she lets me, which is already a relief. "Just tell me what happened," I say, and the words come out even and calm. Deadly calm.

"I feel like… Bastian." Her words are choked as she buries her head in her knees, pulling away from me.

The only thing I focus on is keeping my hands on her. She's here with me. My Chloe Rose is right here, and I've got her.

"Whoever it was just wanted to freak me out, but I don't know how they know about the list unless they overheard at the butcher shop. But I didn't say the names out loud, did I?" Her words come one after the other, stumbling over each other, but the second she's done, she breathes in deep and rubs her eyes. "I know I didn't." She answers her own question before I can say anything. My blood is hot with rage, wanting to know exactly who messaged her and why the fuck they'd get in my way.

Still not looking at me, she apologizes. "I'm sorry."

Frozen and struggling to push the command through clenched teeth, I repeat my question, "Who texted you?" If they're fucking with her, they're fucking with me.

"They said Jeff Adler's dead. I don't know who it is. I don't…" She doesn't finish. Instead, she shakes out her hands and grabs onto her knees, burying her head so she doesn't have to look at me.

My blood runs cold. He's next on the list. She knows it. I know it. Only two left.

With a deep exhalation, she finally looks up at me and she apologizes again. "I'm sorry," she says, and her voice is soft. "I feel like I'm being crazy, but I'm scared."

She has no idea how ridiculous those words are coming from her mouth.

"I saw," I tell her, knowing she needs to be told enough so she thinks it's okay. That everything is okay. "On my way back from Carter's, there's a bunch of people around the site. Looks like a car hit him." Her mouth drops slowly as I give her the partial truth.

"What? No." Her first reaction is denial and she reaches for her phone, but I take it from her, hellbent on finding the number and who it belongs to. "I looked, no one was saying anything."

I don't respond to her and she stays stiff at my side as I look up the number and put it in my own phone. Nothing. Reading the texts, I know who sent it. I just don't know why and every thought that comes up makes my knuckles turn white as I try not to break the fucking phone in my hand.

Anger is a deadly thing.

"He's dead." Her voice shakes with fear and it's that sound that pulls me back to her.

"It was an accident." I'm firm with her, pulling her in closer to me. "Word gets around." I start coming up with an explanation. "I think people know you're freaked is all, Chlo." I feel her eyes on me, but I can't look down at her. If she looks into my eyes, she'll know I'm lying.

I have to stand up and start walking to the bedroom, stripping down and making it look like I'm anything but on the brink of tearing this place apart.

"People know what?" she calls out and I hear her get off the sofa to come after me, her footsteps echoing down the hall.

I need to calm the fuck down. If for no other reason than to calm her down, so she stops thinking about it all. She can't do anything to fuck this up.

With my jaw hard and my back stiff, I turn to her slowly, seeing her prettily framed in the doorway. I force a small smile to my lips. "It's no one, Chlo, but it's okay. I'd be freaked out too. Whoever it was, wasn't thinking."

I have to hide my shock at how well I just lied. How easy it came out. Desperation is an ugly thing.

Her distraught expression slowly fades, replaced with hesitant relief. Her lips stay parted as she lets my words sink in, slowly believing the little lies I'm feeding her.

And it fucking kills me. What I'm doing to her destroys everything in me.

"Come here," I tell her as I tear my shirt off over my head and toss it carelessly on the floor. My three steps take up the entire space of the room as I go to her, wrapping her in my arms and kissing her temple. Her fingers wrap around my forearm and she looks up at me, eyes wide and wanting so badly to believe what I'm telling her.

"I'm sorry you got spooked, but it's nothing. An accident."

"Another coincidence?" she questions me, but her tone isn't a question. My heart thrums and a chill spread over my body.

"It was an accident," I repeat, making my tone a little harder and staring into her eyes until she believes me.

"I don't know... that text and--"

I huff, cutting her off and staring past her. She squirms in my periphery and I'm a fucking asshole. I'm an asshole for making her think this is all in her head.

"This isn't how I wanted tonight to go," I say softly, thinking about last night and how easy it was to get lost in her. If I could live in that moment, I would.

"I'm sorry," she mumbles and her warm breath flows over my skin.

Glancing down at her, I feel like the prick I am. "It's not your fault," I whisper in her hair and then plant a small kiss on her crown. She's so warm in my arms, so small and fragile in so many ways. "I get it, Chlo, but I promise you it's nothing."

She stares deeply into my eyes for what feels like forever and I whisper against her lips, "It's all right, just have faith in me."

She kisses me tenderly, softly, and slowly, even though the pain and worry are still etched in her eyes.

"Come on, let me tell you a story." My hand splays on her back as I lean out into the hallway to turn off the light and then take her to bed.

She crawls in slowly, climbing on top of the sheets before pulling them back and sitting cross-legged where she slept last night.

"My grandmom used to do this thing late at night when she'd come home from work." I latch onto the first story I can think of, so I can occupy her thoughts with something else.

She leans forward slightly, waiting for more and eager to hear what I have to tell her. The way she looks at me with her beautiful blue eyes does something to me and I have to look away.

"Back when I was real little," I say and swallow the lump growing in my throat, "I still remember it."

I settle into the sheets next to her, kicking off my jeans first and flicking on the lamp to cast some light onto her face. When I get into bed, I slip off my watch and it clinks as I set it on the nightstand.

"I never met her," Chloe Rose whispers as she lies down like I'm doing, getting closer to me, and letting me put my arm around her so she can rest her cheek on my chest. Just knowing I have her like this, knowing I can ease her fears and she trusts me... it's everything.

"She worked real late, at least it was late for me."

"Where'd she work?" Chlo asks as I remember how I used to wait up every night for her, but sometimes I couldn't do it.

"At the diner past Walnut. She was a waitress up till the day she died."

Chloe nods and her hair tickles against my chest when she does, but I love it. It brings a comfort that rolls through my chest and I reach up to let my fingers slip through her hair.

"So, I'd wait up every night I could and if I did, she always had something for me. She always had a little gift." My words make Chloe perk up to look at me.

"Like what kind of gift?" She seems far too interested in that detail and it makes me smirk down at her with a huff of humor slipping through my lips.

That bright blush I love to see colors her expression and she finally looks like she might be getting over the text messages, thank fuck. "Sorry, I was just thinking you know how I'd like to get you something for being so nice to me," she confesses and then lets her finger trace up my chest. "I don't know what you like though."

My chest rises as I shrug and say, "You don't have to get me anything."

"I'm fully aware that I don't have to. That doesn't change the fact I *want* to get you something." She gives me a soft smile as she adds, "Thank you, by the way."

"For what?"

"For this," she tells me with that sadness and fear returning to her eyes. I can't respond, knowing what I'm doing, but I don't have to. She kisses my jaw and tells me, "Ignore me, keep going. I like hearing stories. Especially if they're about you."

"You sure you're not going to interrupt as soon as I get going again?" I tease her and instantly feel her smile against my chest. That makes it all right. It makes it all right because she's smiling now and that's what matters.

"Time will tell," is all she says, and I love it. I love all of her.

"So, my grandmom, she'd come home and put her purse down, and I'd get all excited." I glance down at Chlo and get back to running my hand in her hair as I remember what it used to feel like. "I never slept in my room, always the living room so I could hear her when she got in.

"Every time she'd smile down at me, like me waiting

up for her made her the happiest person in the world. And I really believed it too. She'd set everything down and come sit in the recliner, letting me sit on her lap and tell her everything that happened that day at school."

It fucking hurts remembering the small pieces of it that come to me. Things I didn't even know I remembered.

"She'd always have a candy for me. Always. Sometimes there'd be a toy too, something small. Like things you'd get in a piñata."

Chloe hums a small acknowledgment and lifts her leg to lay over mine as she peeks up at me. I pull her in closer, loving that she's letting me tell her this.

"I always thought that she would go get something for me before coming home, you know?" I clear my throat, remembering how some nights if I wasn't able to stay up, I actually felt bad. She'd gone through that trouble of getting me something, and I couldn't even stay up for her. I remember wondering if that was why mom left. Because I didn't stay up for her.

"I was six, I think when she died. And after the funeral, everyone came back to the house." The depth of emotions that play in the soft blues of Chloe's eyes force me to look at the ceiling rather than at her.

"And I didn't know any of the people. I hardly recognized my own mother, because she'd been gone for years, but this one guy, an older guy with glasses, sat down in my grandmom's recliner. And when he did, he pulled up a Zip-loc bag, and it had all the treats in it."

I can feel Chloe's eyes on me, but I can't look down at her. It's so stupid, but I can feel tears pricking my eyes.

"Grandmom had a stash I didn't know about. She didn't pick one out every night. It was right there all along." I clear my throat and tell her, "I kicked him, Chlo. I kicked him hard and grabbed the bag from him. I grabbed it so hard that it tore, and the candy and little toys fell everywhere. They weren't his though. They were Grandmom's. It was her stash to give to me."

I feel the tears on my chest at the same time as I hear Chloe sniffle.

"I'm sorry," she whispers, and I hold her closer to me.

"It's all right, Chlo. Just a story I remembered." I don't tell her the rest. How my mom beat my ass in front of everyone and made me throw away all the candy. She struck me so hard I fell to the floor. I don't tell her how I cried uncontrollably and my mother, who I hadn't seen in years, held my face up for everyone to see that she was punishing her brat of a child who didn't deserve any candy. And that was why she left. That's what she told them. That she was cursed with a bad kid.

She was so proud that everyone got to see her being

the mother she never was. And the only thing I had to hold on to, was that those tears weren't for her. They were never for her.

"Your grandmother sounds like a wonderful person."

"She was," I tell her and we're both quiet for a long time.

"Hey, if you could up and leave, where would you go?" I ask her even though I can see sleep taking her already. She's going to pass out soon and then I need to take care of some shit. I'll be careful; I won't wake her up.

"Anywhere that would take me," she says playfully.

"I'm serious. What would you do?" I ask her, wondering if she's really thought about it. If she'd really run away one day. She props herself up on her elbow, still lying on her stomach and considers me.

"I think I could be a writer. Not like a reporter... but like my books. Fiction."

"If you could do anything at all, you'd write?" It takes me a minute to visualize it. Her bundled up on a sofa, with a mug of tea beside her, jotting down notes or typing away. I could see it. She'd be good at it.

"I feel like that's where I belong, you know? I can kind of be a little weird in person, but when I read or write, it's so freeing."

"I get that," I tell her, feeling a knot growing in my throat. "You could do it, Chlo. You know?" I ask her even though everything in me is telling me not to put those thoughts in her head. I don't want her to run away, I don't want her to leave me.

She gives me a weak smile that mixes with her shyness as she tucks a lock of hair behind her ear before settling back down and yawning.

"And what would you do?" she asks as she nudges me, peeking up at me to add, "If you could do anything."

I think about her question for a long time, long after I shrug and tell her to go to bed. Long after she nuzzles up next to me and falls asleep in my arms. The only answer I can think of is if I could do anything in the world, I'd run away with her.

The only place I want to be is with her.

"Chlo," I whisper her name not long after sleep's taken her from me. Her brow is pinched and the sweet expression on her beautiful face has been replaced by something else. Something that lingers in the place between fear and worry. A small whimper is all I get from her as her nails dig into my arm, holding on to me for dear life. Whatever's got her mind now isn't what I want her thinking about.

The only thing on her mind should be thoughts of us together. It would only be fair since she's the only thing I can think about anymore.

With one hand on her shoulder, I give her a gentle shake to wake her, hard enough to know I'll snap her out of her sleep. "Chloe Rose." I keep my voice gentle and soothing as her wide doe eyes peer up at me, the traces of fear still dancing in her gaze.

Her chest rises and falls with a slow and steadying breath as she looks past me, at the room and then back to my gaze. "You're with me, Chloe Rose." My words are meant to be soothing, but the reaction I get from her is more powerful than I could ever imagine. She pulls herself closer to me, molding every inch of her soft body to mine, kissing my neck, my collar, my chest. Her hands roam down my stomach and then she slips her hand up my chest, letting her fingers play with the small smattering of hair that trails down to my lower half.

The next time I say her name, it's merely a stifled groan. "Chlo." My dick is harder than it's ever been before.

She wants me. She fucking wants me.

"Sebastian," she whispers my name with desperation, brushing her lips against my neck again and letting her kisses trail everywhere they can.

She's in need and so am I.

I roll her over onto her back, and she lets out a small squeal of surprise. It's short-lived as I climb on top of her, kicking off my pants while her fingers spear through my hair and her lips hungrily find mine.

Her tongue brushes against the seam of my lips as I push my fingers inside of her. I have to pull away from the kiss, groaning deep and low in my chest from how hot and wet she is for me already.

"I need you," she whispers and rocks her cunt against my dick.

I don't make her wait, I push myself inside of her, getting harder from the sweet, tortured sounds she gives me in return. She's still so tight, so fucking hot and wet too. It takes me far too long to be buried deep inside of her and when I finally am, giving her a moment to acclimate to my size, her heels dig into my ass, her nails at my back and she begs, fucking begs me, to take her hard.

I give her everything she wants. With one slam of my hips, she screams out my name. Another thrust and she's biting her lip and muffling her cries, but her gaze stays on mine. Those beautiful hues of baby blue swirling with desire, and something else. Something deeper. Something that stirs the beast inside of me to do anything for her, give her anything she ever needs. And to make her mine.

All mine.

Rutting between her legs, I piston my hips, feeling the cold sweat spread along my skin as I hold back my need to cum.

"Bastian," she moans my name as her pussy tightens and her back bows under me.

"Cum for me," I command her in a voice I don't

recognize. One desperate and breathless. One that's just for her.

And she does. She obeys me, instantly spasming on my cock. Her head falls back and her lips part as her orgasm rocks through her.

I don't stop. The second her gaze is off mine, I fuck her harder, ruthlessly, riding through her orgasm and prolonging every bit of it that I can. Dragging it out of her.

She writhes under me and her head thrashes.

My heart beats hard against my chest, feeling hers in time with me.

She's mine. All of her is mine. For always.

Fuck Romano; fuck this city.

I pound into her harder, wanting her to feel every emotion that's raging through me. I'm staying with her.

Her gasp is followed with a strangled moan that fuels me to grip her hips harder, giving her every bit of me.

Nothing's going to keep me from her.

Nothing.

CHLOE

Sebastian's phone keeps going off. I thought it was in my dream at first.

My mother was hissing something. I still hear her words as my eyes flutter open. She said, *He's lying to you.* Her voice keeps me frozen under the warm sheets as the bed dips and Sebastian sits up to grab his phone.

I'm motionless as he moves. She was right here. I can still feel her. She was here.

His voice is groggy as I try to breathe and shake off the eerie feeling that my mother still haunts me in my sleep, even if I can't remember what the dream was.

He's lying to you.

"Yeah, what is it?" Sebastian's voice sounds off. The worry that lingers in his tone grabs my full attention, leaving the thoughts of my mother and whatever had

WILLOW WINTERS

come to me in my sleep where it belongs, in the past. In my unconscious.

"No, no…" He rubs his brow and turns away from me as whoever it is who's called him talks loud enough that I can almost hear the replies on the other end. "I'm sorry," he says with a pained voice, "Yeah, yeah. Are you okay?"

The dread grows as I watch him, how he looks so hurt sitting on the edge of the bed and listening to whoever it is on the other line.

He swallows thickly before saying goodbye and tossing the phone on his nightstand. With his head hung low, I can hear him swallow.

"Who was it?" I dare to ask in a whisper as if speaking too loudly would cause the pain he's feeling to cut even deeper.

I scoot closer to him, but slowly as he lifts his head to answer, "Carter."

My stomach twists into a knot, just like the one in my heart as Bastian adds, "His mom died."

My throat is tight as the swell of sadness rises. I didn't know her at all, but I knew the end had to be closer after she was moved into their house for hospice.

It's devastating to lose your mother, whether you know it's coming or not.

"So much death." The words escape me slowly as I tally up the number of gravestones.

202

"I care more about him than any of those assholes." Bastian's tone is harsh and unforgiving. I peek over at him as he rubs the sleep from his eyes angrily, his feet on the floor while he still sits on the bed. I've never seen him look so tired, so ragged from everything and the pain of it all forces me to move closer to him, pushing the sheets and covers away to just hold him. I rest my cheek to his back and wrap my arms around him from behind.

"I'm sorry," I whisper against his back and then lift myself up, so I can plant a small kiss on his neck. "I'm so sorry," I tell him again.

I don't know how close he was with Carter's mom, but it doesn't matter. He's hurting. Lacing his fingers through mine, he kisses my inner wrist. "Are you okay?" he asks me, turning his head so he can look me in the eyes. Of all the things to ask, he wants to know if I'm all right.

His eyes are red with lack of sleep, his stubble is too long, and there are dark bags under his eyes as well. I have to slip my hand from his to cup his cheek and sit up to kiss him on his lips. A chaste, sweet kiss. My heart flutters every time I kiss him. It's an odd feeling, like a magnetic pull to him.

I brush his lips with the pad of my thumb and whisper to him, "It's not always about me, Bastian." With his name on my lips, I look him in the eyes and say, "I'll be okay."

"You're wrong," he tells me, shifting to sit so he's facing me. "It is always about you."

His answer steals my breath, numbing me as he kisses my wrist again.

"You shouldn't say things like that." I can't help but tell him as the words come to me.

His steely blue eyes catch me off guard; they pierce into me and hold me hostage as he asks, "And why is that?"

"You make me feel like I'm more to you than I am." The words come unbidden, his simple question enough to draw the raw truth from me. I lick my lips as I blink away the haze of the spell he casts over me. Bringing my knees into my chest, I scoot away from him and wish I could take those words back.

"You're wrong again," he tells me, and I feel foolish.

"I know I'm an easy lay," I tell him dully, feeling my heart squeeze in my chest. I would let him have me whenever he wanted.

"I didn't say you were. I don't do this; I don't sleep around. I don't have girls stay over, so we're even there. So, whatever you're thinking right now, stop it."

Guilt rises inside of me and makes me feel sick to my stomach. This is not the time, nor the place. I can feel his gaze on me, I know he's waiting for me to simply agree and so I swallow the spiked knot and nod, but I can't look him in the eyes.

"You know you mean more to me than that. You're

more than that." His conviction is unmistakable, but I don't know that. I only know what he's told me, which is nothing.

He never tells me anything and I let him into my life because that's where I want him. It's as simple as that.

Taking a steadying breath, I turn to him.

"Tell me you know that," he commands me, and my eyes are drawn to his throat as he swallows. "Tell me you know you're more than just a lay for me."

"I do," I tell him. Things have always been *more* between us, but why? I don't know. And tomorrow holds no promises for me.

"I want to have someone, Bastian," I confess to him. "Even if I may lose them one day. I don't want to be alone anymore." I don't know where the words come from. Maybe it's the fatigue that still lingers. The sadness from hearing of Carter's mom passing. Or maybe it's because I feel a crack in Sebastian's armor, he's giving me a way in to tell him exactly how I feel.

It's too quiet as I stare straight ahead at nothing in particular, rather than at Sebastian.

He cups the side of my face and forces me to look at him. His touch is hot and his gaze even hotter as he tells me, "Then let me be that someone."

My heart beats in slow motion.

"What am I to you?" I whisper. Because deep in my soul, I already know Sebastian is that person for me.

What I don't know is whether or not I'm that person for him.

"You were just the sad girl who looked at me like you couldn't wait to run from me. So, I refused to chase you, Chloe. Now that I have you, I'm begging you, don't run from me."

I love you is on the tip of my tongue, but the strength to let the words be heard is nowhere to be found.

"People know you're with me now, anyway," he tells me when I don't say anything. "There's nowhere to run."

"I want to run away from here. I don't know that I can stay here, Bastian." I don't know why that's what comes out of me, but it's all I can say.

His answer is simple and unexpected. "When you figure out where, tell me."

His hand falls from my cheek and he gets off the bed, making my body sway where it is. My gaze drifts to him, watching him stand at the dresser and open a drawer, and then to the faint light of early morning filtering in through the window.

"Where are you going?" I ask him and then add, "To Carter's?" He only nods solemnly. Of course, he'd want to be with him. I'm sure Carter needs him there too.

"Do you want me to go with you?" I offer. I'd do anything for him.

"You keep looking for a way to run from me, Chloe

Rose," he says and although he isn't facing me as he slips on a white cotton t-shirt, I can hear the smile that must be gracing his lips, "but I need you this time. You're not allowed to leave now."

"So, that's a yes?" I push him for more, feeling a warmth spread through my body and cloaking the sadness still buried within.

"It's a, 'you should have known you're coming with me.'"

SEBASTIAN

I knew it was coming. We all did. But we're dying every day, coming closer to the end of our time here on earth, and it's never easy to accept.

It's been four days since she passed. And four days of Carter not calling. I keep texting him, but he just gives me one-word answers. His dad was right, nothing can prepare you; I didn't think Carter would push me away though, not when he needs someone there for him. Even if it's just to sit around and do nothing, I don't care what, I just want to be there for him.

But he has his brothers.

Let me know when I can come over, I text him. And it takes a few minutes with only the sound of the paper bags rustling from Chlo getting the Chinese food out before Carter replies that he will.

I think he's lying though. I don't think he's going to ask for help or for anyone to come around. He's not okay.

"You should go to him," Chloe speaks up, dishing out the lo mein on both of the paper plates with the white plastic forks they threw in the bag. "I think he'd like that," she adds. She's on her knees in front of the coffee table in nothing but a shirt of mine.

Tossing my phone on the sofa, I get down on the floor with her. It's awkward and I have to push the coffee table away a foot, so I can fit between it and the sofa.

The sound of her small laugh soothes a piece of me that's hurting for Carter. I peer up at her with a smirk on my lips. "Not everyone's a tiny little thing like you," I tell her and watch that soft blush creep up in her cheeks.

"I love making you smile," I say and it only makes her blush harder. She bites down on her lip, reaching for another carton. She dishes out the General Tso's quietly until both plates have more than enough on them.

"I love it when you make me smile too," she says sheepishly, sitting back on her heels. "But seriously," she tells me, "I think he'd be happy if you stopped by."

"Yeah," I agree with her, remembering how she was at Carter's house and then at the funeral. She was quiet and polite, but the moment someone was ready to break down, she was right there. For Carter, but for Daniel too, his younger brother. All she wanted to do was be there to take away the pain as much as she could.

I love her for it.

I love her for being her.

She peeks up at me as the thought occurs to me, but she quickly looks away and repositions herself. She's barely eating, just pushing the food around on her plate.

"What's wrong?" I ask her, a nagging feeling inside of me that what we have is going to go away. It's all going to slip through my fingers and I'm going to lose her.

She clears her throat and glances at me, her gaze shifting between the untouched plate and then back to me. I have to put my fork down and push the plate away to face her. "Tell me what's wrong."

"I think I love you." Her answer is immediate, although each word feels hesitant like it was afraid to be spoken. "I think I'm weird and needy... and that I have problems," she says then swallows thickly, and the blush that was on her face turns a darker shade of red before she looks up at me again with those blue eyes shining with vulnerability. "But I think I love you, and I don't know if... if it's okay that I tell you." She bites down on her bottom lip and then nods once like she's said her piece. "But I wanted to tell you," she adds quickly before I can answer her.

She'll never know how she breaks something inside of me with her confession. With how genuine and sincere those words come out. I know she means it. She feels that she loves me, and she loves the part of me she knows. It shatters something deep down inside of me. The part of me that's hiding from her sight, the part of me I hate, that part of me falls to my knees for her, praying I could atone for all my sins and be worthy of that love.

"Lie down, Chloe Rose," I give her the command, feeling my heart slamming against my chest, begging me to tell her how I feel. I'm not ready though. I love seeing her squirm, and a part of me thinks if she knew how much she meant to me, she'd run.

She glances at me warily before setting her fork down and scooting out from between the coffee table and the sofa to lie down on her side only to ask, "On my back?"

Letting out a single huff of a laugh, I grin at her and say, "Yeah."

With her heels on the floor and her knees bent, she lies on her back, the t-shirt riding up and she lets it, so I can see her underwear.

"Take them off," I tell her from where I'm sitting, feeling my cock get harder for her. Pulling her hair behind her first, she obeys me. Shimmying out of her

underwear and setting it next to her, she daintily readjusts so her legs are flat and I can't see her cunt.

"Like you were before, Chloe Rose. I want to
see you."

Slowly, she picks up each of her heels, her pussy on
full display, her center a dark, bright pink and glis-
tening from arousal.

"Tell me you love me again."

She brings her gaze to meet mine and licks her lips.
"I love you," she tells me like it's obvious. Like it doesn't
change anything at all.

I have to practically crawl to her from where I'm
sitting, but I don't give a fuck.

I don't need food; I don't need sleep. I don't need a
damn thing, so long as she loves me.

With a single finger, I push on her inner knees and
she instantly moves her legs farther apart for me. I
trace her pussy, sending shivers through her body.

"So, does that mean you're my girlfriend?" I ask her
the question I wanted to so many years ago. If I hadn't
already been involved with Romano, heading down a
path I knew she was too good for, I'd have asked her
then. Shit, I'd have begged her to be mine.

The corners of her lips turn up as she smiles wide
and beautifully. "Yeah," she answers me in a single
breath and I reward her by brushing the rough pad of
my thumb over her swollen clit. Her sweet, soft moan

makes precum leak from the slit of my cock and I can't take it anymore.

She watches as I undress fast and recklessly, kicking the coffee table and almost spilling the food, but it doesn't matter. None of that shit matters.

She spreads her legs farther as I climb on top of her, bracing my forearms on either side of her head and kissing her softly, gently and giving her every ounce of goodness, I have, even if it is so little.

"You still sore, Chlo?" I ask her as I push into her slick folds just enough to feel her tight cunt gripping my cock before pulling out.

With her neck arched back, her lips parted, and her eyes closed, she whimpers, "No."

"Good," I tell her, "'Cause tomorrow you're going to be." I slam into her all the way to the hilt in a swift, merciless stroke. Her sweet gasps fuel me to fuck her on the thin carpet until she doesn't have a scream left in her.

CHLOE

"*I loved coming here.*" *My mother's voice is calm and sober, which is at odds with the noise of the bottles clinking and everyone talking in the bar. It sounds like everyone's talking at once and over each other. The billiard balls collide on the break and the sound of a new game starting draws my attention briefly. The television's on with a football game and some of the guys cheer a player on, but he the whole bar voices its dismay as he's quickly tackled.*

I recognize a few faces, one of them Carter's dad as he orders a drink.

"That man's going soon." My mother's voice catches my attention. Goosebumps flow over my skin; she's so close to me. A thin, sickly smile is on her lips. She nods, not taking her gaze away from the far end of the bar as we sit on two stools next to each other.

I look back to the man I recognize and ask, "Mr. Cross?"

"No, no, baby girl," my mother tsks me, "the bartender."

Dave.

Ice flows over my skin as my mom laughs at my reaction. Fifth on the list.

The billiard balls clack noisily, and the bar carries on like nothing's happening. Like they can't even see us.

Sharp nails dig into my shoulder as my mom comes closer to me, whispering in my ear and making my body stiffen.

"I used to fuck him at the end of the night," she tells me with her smile growing. "He'd clear my tab in return, although sometimes he just wanted me to suck him off like a whore."

My words fail me and I struggle to breathe or to know what to say. It's only a dream.

"Yeah, yeah, baby girl. But that doesn't make it any less true," my mom tells me before letting go and sitting upright in her seat.

I swallow the tight knot in my throat and peek up at her.

"Just because you're dreaming doesn't mean shit." The smile fades and she stares at the bartender as he pours a glass of some clear liquor for Mr. Cross.

The music seems to die down, everything except my mother's voice turning to white noise.

"At one point, I thought he loved me," my mom tells me, staring down at the drink on the bar.

It takes me a moment to realize the smudge on the glass is blood. My gaze darts to her hand, to the broken nails and the bruises on her wrist.

My heart pounds, the anxiety and fear rising as her voice hardens and she picks up the drink. "Men don't love, Chloe." She sets the glass against her lips, but she doesn't drink. Instead, she stares at the man behind the bar. She stares down the bartender who doesn't see either of us. "Don't you ever believe that shit."

I grip the barstool tighter, feeling the blood draining from me as she looks me in the eyes, her own pale and lifeless. "Don't believe him, Chloe Rose."

I WAKE UP DRENCHED in sweat and alone. Trembling, I can hear the faint sounds of someone outside. I can't help getting out of bed, my heart still racing as I check to see who it is.

Peeking through the blinds, it's just two guys walking down the street. Guys I've seen before on the porch of a house down the street. They look like they're on their way back from the liquor store, carrying bags full of large glass bottles. That would explain the noises I heard in my sleep.

I'm still shaking as I turn from the window and slowly walk back to the bed, my mind racing with the memory of the dream. Of the bar. Of Dave.

I reach out to Bastian's side of the bed, but the sheets are cold.

Blinking the sleep from my eyes, I walk to the bathroom, my bare feet padding against the cold floor. The door's partially open and it's dark inside, but still, I push it open wide and flick on the light.

The brightness makes me wince, and I find it empty.

"Bastian?" I call out for him even though I know he's not here. His place is empty.

Where the hell is he? The clock on the stove reads 3:46. "Where the fuck is he?" I mutter, still breathless from the fear that woke me. I'd rather focus on Bastian than on the night terror, but when I get to my phone that I'd left on the coffee table, my blood runs cold.

Dave now too. They're going one by one.

I stare at the text message, reading it over and over.

Dave is dead.

I dreamed of it. And he's dead. I'm so cold. I can't feel anything but the horror I felt from the nightmare.

I don't know how I'm still standing. The scream of fear is silent in my throat, but it's there.

Tears prick my eyes and I can't control the shaking. Adrenaline and the need to run kick in before I can do anything. It all happens so slowly, each level of despair falling on its own. Like dominoes. And between each blow, I reread the text.

Dave now too. They're going one by one.

My knees collapse, and I drop the phone, pressing my hands together and begging them to stop shaking.

It was a dream. She's not real.

It's not real. Tell me the text isn't real. It's not true.

It's just some asshole fucking with me. There's no truth to it.

I swallow each of the thoughts, pushing my head into the carpet and trying to steady my head from spinning with the fear racing through me.

But how can it be a coincidence? It can't. It can't be. It's not real.

"Bastian," I cry out for him like the crutch he is. The panic is slow to set in.

I know he'll make it better. He's a balm each and every time. He can make it go away.

But he can't explain this. Nothing can explain this.

I reach for my phone and miss it, but then I grab it again, my nails digging into the carpet as I drag it closer to me. "Pull your shit together," I mutter under my breath. I lift my gaze to the front door as I scroll for Sebastian's number.

My body is hot, and tense and the fear threatens to consume me.

It's locked. The door is locked.

Ring, ring, ring.

No answer.

I stare at the screen as if it's lying to me. I don't

know how long I sit there on my knees, my ass on my heels as I stare at the fucking phone, hating it and hating this place and freezing. I'm so cold. I'm so fucking cold.

It was a nightmare, it's not real.

I try again and get the same result, voicemail.

Swallowing thickly, I brave looking at the text message again.

I could ask who it is, but they won't tell me.

I could ask for proof, but I don't want to see.

Instead, I try Sebastian again because he's all I have. And still, I get nothing. My heart races and the anxiety grows inside me, burning me from the inside out and nearly shoving me over the brink of insanity.

It's okay, I tell myself as I rock on the floor. *It's okay.*

It's just a nightmare. Just a text.

Just another coincidence.

"Bastian," I cry out for him and feel so unworthy. So unhinged.

Where is he?

He has to be with Carter, out on the edge of the city where there's no reception. It's my fault. I told him to go there. It's my fault, I repeat to myself.

Finally, my body moves. I need to get dressed and go to him. I can't stay here. I won't do it. I need to tell him; I need to tell someone. I'm breaking down and I don't know what to do. I don't know what's real.

I'm not crazy.

A scream tears through me as the phone rings in my hand. I drop it, the vibrations feeling like fire against my skin.

It rings again, and I see it's Sebastian.

My fingers shake as I answer it and wait for his voice.

"Chlo?" he asks, and I struggle to put what's going on into words.

"I need you," is all I manage. I can barely breathe.

"Chloe, it's okay." I hear the tone of his voice morph from curious to concerned. "What's wrong?" he asks me.

"I had a nightmare," I cover my mouth with my wrist, remembering my mom and her words.

"Chlo, it's just a dream," he tells me as tears prick my eyes.

"I dreamed about Dave and then I got a text," I push the words out and take in a deep breath. Shaking out my other hand, and staring straight ahead at the stark white wall, I wait for him to say something that makes sense, something that will make me feel better.

"I'll be there soon," he tells me, and I nod my head, my throat raw with emotion.

"I'm not okay," I tell him in strangled words.

"It'll be all right," is his only answer before the line goes dead. But it's not all right. It's not going to be all right. I wanted them all to die for having done nothing while my mother cried out for help. I wanted them to feel the pain and regret that I felt every damn day for years when I cried myself to sleep. They felt nothing, and it wasn't fair. That was years ago though and I don't want this. I would never ask for this now.

I'm living in my own hell.

SEBASTIAN

I hang up the call and stare at the dirt and blood on my hand that's holding the phone.

"I need to shower at your place before I go home," I call out to Carter who's still leaning against his father's beat-up truck.

My hands are numb and yet they still burn from the blisters that'll come tomorrow. I don't know what I'll tell Chlo if she notices them. The shovel did a number on me and it all proved for shit.

"You hear me?" I ask him, my voice barely carrying into the early morning darkness.

"Yeah." Carter's answer is weak. He looks like shit. He looks like he just lost it and that makes sense. 'Cause that's exactly what happened.

The river babbles in the night along with the sound

of the crickets. It's all I can hear as the sun starts to peek over the horizon.

Another night with no sleep and another night with Chloe falling apart. She knows too much.

"You ready?" he asks me before pounding his fist so hard into the truck I swear he's going to dent it. He's losing it. He can't hold himself together.

The dew on the grass soaks into my jeans as I walk through the tall grass to the truck.

I grab his shoulder, shaking him. "It's over with; it's done." I'm firm with him even though my heart is pounding recklessly.

Carter nods his head but immediately throws up. He vomits off the side of the truck with both hands on his upper thighs. The smell is rancid, and I can't stand to be around it.

I feel fucking sick to my stomach too. I hate this. I hate this life.

I lay a hand on his back, patting him hard once before walking away from him and climbing into the driver's side. The truck rocks as I do, and I can't shake the eerie feeling that I'm being fucked over.

He texted her again. I'm blocking that fucking number. He crossed a line doing that shit, and I don't give a fuck who he is. I won't let him get to her. My Chloe is off-limits. There's no exception to that.

It wasn't supposed to happen this way, but it doesn't matter. He knows. I know he knows.

Laying my head back against the leather headrest, I wait for Carter, looking over my shoulder and watching him wipe his mouth with the sleeve of his shirt. He takes it off, leaving on his t-shirt underneath and throws it into the back of the truck before getting in.

The rusty door closes with a protest, right before slamming shut with finality.

"I'm sorry," he tells me as he looks out the window. I feel bad for him; more than anything, I feel fucking awful for the kid. I can handle Chloe. I'll figure it out for her, but this fucked him up.

"You're all right," I tell him and then swallow the rest of the thought. "It's fine."

It's this place. How many times have I said that recently? Crescent Hills is a living – waking – nightmare for everyone in it. Only the devil himself could live here and feel at peace.

"I have to tell Marcus he's here, but I won't tell anyone else, all right?" The truck rumbles as I start it up. Carter looks like he's going to lose his shit again; he's still shaking.

"It's just the adrenaline," I tell him, to try to calm him down.

He peeks up at me, the early morning light making his worn expression look that much more ragged. "I killed him," he tells me again. I can't count how many times he's told me that tonight.

Nodding at him, I look in the rearview at the river where I ditched Dave's body before putting the truck into drive.

"He was going to die anyway," I tell Carter although I stare straight ahead at the dirt road rather than looking at him again. "His name was on the list."

CHLOE

*I*f Dave is dead, Andrea is next.

And then me.

There are no coincidences like this, and I can't just wait around to be a sitting duck. I can't ignore it any longer. I can't pretend to be okay and walk through this life as if I'm only a ghost. It's what I've done for as long as I can remember, and maybe weeks ago, I would have prayed for the end to come quickly and peacefully.

But I'm not ready to go. I don't want to die.

I want to run away from all of this.

I want to be free of it all.

I want more than this shit life.

More than anything, I want Sebastian to come with me.

The front door to his house opens, and I don't wait

for him to speak. "There's something wrong with me," I tell him, feeling every inch of my throat go dry and the pit in my stomach growing heavier and heavier. I heave the words up my throat. "Someone is killing them and if you don't believe me, that's fine." The last word cracks as I feel myself unraveling.

Sebastian stays by the door, completely still and watching me, watching as I transform into a lunatic in front of him. I don't know what he thinks of all this, of how often I'm nothing but an emotional mess. The nightmares, the list. I can't imagine what he thinks, he always brushes it aside, but I can't do it any longer.

"I can't pretend it's a coincidence."

He finally speaks, low and with a note of apprehension, "What brought this on? The text?"

My body is ice cold as I sit on the sofa, pulling my knees into my chest and refusing to look him in the eyes. "I don't think it's someone messing with me." I dare to peek up at him, willing him to feel the very real fear that keeps me on the edge of sanity.

"I wish I could kill him. Whoever it is that's fucking with you."

It shreds me inside to hear the pain in his voice. "I'm not crazy," I beg him to understand.

"I wrote that list, Bastian. I wrote it." The confession is so close, it's begging to come out and be brought to life. With each word scarring its way through my chest, I give in to the weight of it. "And my name was on that list. I wanted them dead and I wanted to die," I tell him as the tears prick at the back of my eyes and I hold myself closer.

Tears leak down my cheek as I rest my heated face against my knee. "I don't want to die," I repeat the one thing I know to be true right now, even if that hasn't always been the case.

"Shh," Bastian shushes me, coming closer and sitting next to me on his sofa. I'll never know how he so easily comforts me, how he doesn't hesitate to wipe my tears away and pull me into his arms. When I'm like this, on the brink of insanity.

"I'm not crazy," I whisper and wonder if it's true.

He rocks me as I gasp for air and try to force the crying to stop. "It's my fault they died," I whisper the harsh truth and his rocking stops, but then continues. My heart races, needing him to tell me something. Anything. To tell me I'm not crazy and that he'd run away with me. That's what I want more than anything.

"Please," I beg him, but I don't have the strength to voice the only thing I've ever wanted.

"There's nothing on the news about Dave," he tells me after a long moment. My head shakes, wanting him to listen to me and believe me. I don't care what's on the news; I know what I feel in my gut.

"I need you to believe me." I try to convince him as I say, "I can feel it. I know it. Whoever it is, they aren't lying."

I'm holding him so tightly; my knuckles turn white. "I can't go to the cops, and I can't run from whoever it is. I feel helpless, Bastian." I've felt helpless for so long and there's only so much a person can take before it turns to hopelessness. "I don't know what to do." The last words are barely spoken. All that lives inside of me now is true fear.

"You need to relax," he tells me softly, but his steely eyes aren't cold. They hold so much sympathy that it nearly makes me break. As if there was any piece of me still whole.

"I can't explain this without sounding crazy," I tell him, although I can't look him in the eyes when I say it. I wipe at my face, hating how weak I am. I would give anything to be strong. "I could wait for the night to come. I have my gun--"

"Chlo, stop it," he warns me, his tone threatening.

"I could try to--"

"Stop it!" he yells at me, so loudly, it shakes me. My body's trembling as I try to get a grip. I have no one and no idea when it's coming. There's one more person before me if Dave is really dead. That's all I know.

"I don't want to live here anymore."

"Then what do you want to do?" he asks me with a hard look that would force me to be silent if it were on anyone else's face.

"I want to run away... for good." My body is numb as I hold my breath, waiting for him to say anything at all, but my chest squeezes with a new kind of pain when he says nothing.

"Please say something," I beg him.

"You have no idea what lengths I would go for you. But you need to stop this, please. Don't do this. Please, Chlo, for me." His words are a plea that rubs salt in the sharpest and deepest wounds I have.

"You don't understand." I take in a quick breath and then another, feeling lightheaded as I confess, "I heard my mom screaming for help and did nothing. I did nothing." I search his eyes for understanding, but also for the hate I felt for myself so long ago. "Whoever is killing them... if it has to do with her... they're going to come for me."

"Chloe, please," he tries to silence me, to brush it off again and I push his arm away instead of accepting the comfort that comes with his touch.

"I don't feel safe here," I tell him while backing away. "I won't stay here any longer." The words themselves are both freeing and suffocating.

I've never belonged here; I've always wanted a way out.

But I've always belonged to Sebastian. In every way. And the idea of running, to never see him again, is the most painful thing I could ever feel.

"Please," I beg him, not just to understand but to come with me.

"If you can't come with me," I try to be strong, to

force the words out, but instead I turn into a blubbering fool. Covering my heated face with both of my hands, I feel the tears burn into my flesh.

"I'll never let you leave me," he tells me, and it only makes me cry harder. Because I don't want him to let me go, I want him to come with me. I need him to come with me. "I don't want to leave you." I gasp for air and give him a singular truth in a despite whisper, "I can't leave you."

He pulls me in close to him, even though I'm no help at all, covering my face and ashamed of what I've become.

"I just need time," he answers me and my head shakes of its own accord.

"I can't... I can't stay here anymore." The last words come out strangled as tears prick my eyes. I can't stay, but I can't leave without him either.

I swear I could be a better person. I could be happy and sane. But not here. All I am here is a name on a list. Waiting for my death.

"I love you, Chloe. I love you." Sebastian's voice is soothing as he wraps both of his arms around me. I crave his touch so much that I bury my head into his chest. He whispers, "I can take you away. We can leave tomorrow."

My body stills, my heart beating far too loud to be sure of what I heard. *Please, let me have heard right.* I can barely manage to swallow as I look into his steely blue eyes, praying he's telling me the truth and not just saying what he knows I want to hear.

He kisses my hair and then brushes it away from my face as he repeats himself, "I can run away with you."

"I love you, Bastian. I love you." The words tumble from my lips. "Please tell me you're telling the truth." I interlock my fingers with his, needing to feel him and know that he means it. "I want to run away with you."

"I love you," he tells me, his gaze never straying from mine, "we can't stay here. I can't stay here anymore."

SEBASTIAN

I did this to her.

But I wouldn't take it back.

I wouldn't take it back because I have her now. I'll run away with her, as far as she wants. I'll hold her every night and watch her fall asleep in my arms.

Always.

She'll never be without me again.

"Is there anyone you still want to talk to?" I ask her as I figure out every detail. Every single thing that has to be done before we leave. She's nestled in the crook of my arm in my bed, her small frame curved around my side. Her hair brushes my arm while she shakes her head. "No," she whispers. Clearing her throat, she adds, "I just want to leave."

I know she does. She's always wanted to leave. Ever

since the first day I met her, I knew I'd run away with her if I could.

"I want you to leave your phone," I tell her, and she asks quickly, "Because of the person who texted about Dave?"

"Partly," I tell her honestly, feeling the anxiety spike inside of me. I don't want her to know the truth. I'll never tell her all of the truth. Never. "I don't know who it is. And I don't like that." I play the possessive card, although I'm sure she can see right through it. "If there's no one you want to call, I'd rather you just leave it behind."

She's quiet for a moment, but instead of asking questions, she concedes. "I can leave it behind. I can leave everything behind." I release a breath I didn't know I was holding and stroke her hair.

"There are a few things I have to do tomorrow. I'll run into work, come back, pack and then we leave." Adrenaline is coursing through me, knowing this is a decision I can't go back on. Once I leave, that's it. There's no coming back and I have no idea where we'll run to.

"Just like that?" she asks with slight disbelief, peeking up at me through her lashes.

"Just like that," I tell her and bend down to kiss her, listening to the bed groan in time with a faint siren from outside. No more streetlights drifting through the window, no more yelling down the street. No more of this city and the people in it. Wherever we go, I want it to be quiet and far, far away from here. I need somewhere we can escape to where no one will find us and where it'll feel like home.

"It's all going to be okay," I whisper against her hair before planting a small kiss on her forehead. She holds me tightly, like she'll never let me go. "It's all going to be all right."

"Promise me you'll run with me?" she asks me again like I'll back out of it.

"Tomorrow we pack up everything in one car," I tell her firmly, "and we leave." I'll do it. I'll leave it all behind to be with her and keep her safe.

"And we leave forever, promise me?" her voice begs me, and I swear I'd give her anything I could. Anything and everything I ever have will be hers.

She's tense at my side, waiting for my answer. I know there's no going back, but I choose her. It's always been her.

"As long as you love me forever," I give her my one condition, feeling the tension in my heart, needing her to agree and say she's mine forever.

"I can make that promise," she breathes, "I'll love you forever."

"I've always loved you," I whisper against her cheek. And it's true. There have never been truer words spoken.

* * *

I TURN NINE TOMORROW. I think, anyway. I want to ask the guy behind the counter, so I'll know for sure. I don't know why I care; I just want to know, I guess.

Peeking over my shoulder, I make sure Jim and my mom are occupied so I can go ask what day it is.

We just moved here. Mom took me with her, although part of me wishes she'd left me at Grandmom's, even if there's no one there anymore. At least I have the memories there. This city is different, everyone's always watching me. Looking at me like I'm going to do something so they can pick a fight.

They say I'm a bad kid. They say I'm angry.

I used to think they were wrong, but I don't anymore.

Boys like me are trouble. Too tall for my age, too smart for my own good. I'm not worth the air I breathe. That's Jim's new saying. He likes to remind me every chance he gets, even though he's the one giving my mom that shit that makes her go numb. He's the one who isn't worth the air he breathes but saying that only gets me punched in the face until I go numb too and black out.

I pull out the candy from my pocket. I only have two pieces left and as I pull out my hand, both of them drop to the floor and one rolls faster than I can catch it.

The candy stops rolling when it hits the edge of the counter and bounces off, only to stop in front of a small pair of shoes. They're white but scuffed up and I slowly lift my gaze to the owner of the shoes. To the short girl who's bending down to pick up my candy.

She can't have it!

My jaw's hard, and I clench my teeth even though the bruise there makes it hurt. My hands turn to fists. All I have left of my grandmom are these two pieces.

She can't have it!

She picks it up so delicately and carefully, then smooths out her dress. It's then that I notice how dirty it is like she's been sitting on the ground all day. It's wrinkled too. When she stands up her big doe eyes are filled with worry and she turns to look at a woman by the fridge doors. The woman's skinny, skinny like my mom. That's what I think as the bottles she's picking up clink together.

The girl looks like she wants to say something, but she's scared, so she says nothing. Her gaze drops to the ground, then she lifts her head back up to look around.

She's looking for me; I know she is.

The instant she sees me, the worry goes away and she smiles. A genuine smile that's just for me.

"Is this yours?" she offers in a soft voice that makes the anger go away. Only for a second though, because the moment she asks me, she peeks over at the woman and looks nervous to even be talking to me.

Because I'm a bad kid. That's why. Everyone knows it. Even her.

Her knees nearly buckle as she stands there, holding the candy out to me even though I'm feet away from her.

She's afraid to move. "My mom told me to stay here," she explains.

I nod and swallow the lump in my throat. She looks sad like me until she smiles at me, then it changes everything.

She's strange. Like she doesn't want to be here.

I may not belong here, but she doesn't either.

"Thanks," I tell her as I walk to her and she nervously looks between me and the woman again, her mom.

She's shy as she talks to me. "I haven't met you before." And then she smiles again, even sweeter this time. She smiles at me like her happiness was meant to belong to me. Like I could take that happiness from her. Like I could be happy too. "I'm Chloe Rose."

CHLOE

*M*aybe if I leave, the nightmares will go away.

Places hold memories. They can't help it. The image of a dented brass doorknob comes to mind. I'll never forget the memory of what put that dent into the hard metal. The sound of a click against a window, the window he crept through late at night. It can't help but exist, yet it carries so much heaviness with it. So much more than just an object, so much more than just a place.

I'm done crying; I'm done remembering.

I think I've been ready to leave for a long time. Longer than the time that first light went out on the street and I had the urge to run in such a primitive way. I think I was ready to run the first time Bastian's lips pressed against mine. My heart knew it, but it would only beat if he came with me.

There's a method to the way I place each item in the old duffle bag. I was given the bag in gym class one year in high school. It was a promotion for some sports drink and I think it could carry at least two weeks' worth of clothes. That's all I need.

Each piece fits in easily. My books I can put in a cardboard box and place in the back. I'll always need my books.

Other than my clothes, I don't know what I'll take. Toiletries, obviously. But these photographs aren't mine and the ones I have, I don't want.

The light catches the glass of a photo on the far right of the wall. A photo of my mother when she was young, and I was in her arms. I don't remember that far back, but my uncle said she loved me deeply. That she bundled me up in that picture because it was so cold out and she was worried about taking me outside for the photos.

She loved me once.

But she loved the alcohol more.

I'm okay with it. I'm okay with it all. Because I survived, and I still know how to love. A piece of me will always love her. I'll love the woman in this photo because she's not the woman in my nightmares.

My fingertips brush along the edges of the frame as my throat tightens and I wish I could go back to that time to tell her. I wish I could go back to so much.

You can only move forward, a voice tells me, and I close my eyes, letting the last tears fall. They linger on my lashes as I open my eyes again and say goodbye to her, leaving the photo where it is.

I carelessly brush them away, gazing at the full duffle bag as my phone pings. It's only one of two people. I already know that.

Please tell me you're okay. I read the text message from Angie and my heart sinks. I think I would have been good friends with her. Even though neither of us ever belonged here. I'm grateful to leave, but I don't know how much this place will take from her before she walks away, if she can even walk away.

I don't know why she'd stay here any longer than she has to. But it's her choice, and she knows what she's doing. Maybe me leaving will push her to run; I try to justify leaving her in the dark with the thought of her being warned to stay away with my disappearance. I can only hope that's what she does.

There's not a damn thing good that lives in Crescent Hills.

Answer me, she texts me, but I don't text her back. The next time it pings, I turn off the phone without looking.

Bastian said it's better to just disappear and for no one to know where we've gone. He's right, and I don't want anyone to come looking for me. If I could disappear and be lost in the wind with Bastian forever, I would. Tonight, I'm going to try to do just that.

I leave the phone on the bed, on the sheets that never belonged to me. It can stay there and when the men come and take everything inside because the bills go unpaid, they can have it.

They can have every piece of what's here.

It never belonged to me and I'm done belonging to it.

SEBASTIAN

I can't stop staring at the note on the counter. It's only a Post-it with the words, "Leaving for the weekend – Seb" written on the yellow square. Eddie will get it on Monday, or maybe this weekend if anyone comes in. The shop is supposed to be empty, with most of the guys going down to the docks for Romano this weekend. There's a large order of coke coming in. And the butcher shop isn't needed for that.

I'll leave a note and I'll ghost. He can try to find me all he wants, but I'm done with Romano and this place. Just as the thought hits me, I hear the bells chime at the front door and a chill seeps into my veins.

"Eddie," I greet him with a grin, hiding the fact that I didn't want anyone to know I was leaving until I was gone. I didn't want anyone to ask questions. "What are you doing here?" I ask and casually lean against the counter. The spool of butcher's cord is right below me. All of us who work in the shop are familiar with it; we use it to secure packages and orders.

I don't reach for it yet, but with the pounding of my blood, I know it's going to end like this. The desire to get it over with forces a numbness through my fingers and I shake it off, smiling as he answers me.

"What am I doing? How about, what the fuck are you doing here?" He shoots me a twisted grin as if he's being friendly, but the look in his eyes is filled with the psychotic glee he's known for. "I heard Romano wants to talk to you," he adds as he walks to the counter, the sound of his boots slapping against the floor in time with the pounding of my heart. He tosses the keys to the shop down on the counter and leans closer to me just as I reach for the cord.

I wind it over my fingers under the counter. The dumb fuck is so hellbent on letting me know my days are numbered in the darkened butcher shop that he doesn't realize his own imminent demise is only a moment away.

"Seems he thinks you have something to do with those assholes coming up dead," he tells me, eyeing me and then glancing out the window as the headlights of a passing car shine through the glass.

Dread rips through me, thinking it's someone else and I won't have time to finish Eddie off, but it's not. The lights flash and keep on going, heading down to the mechanic shop behind us.

"Why would he think that?" I ask him, wrapping the rope around once more and then starting on the other hand. I leave less than a foot of cord between the two. Enough to get the thin rope over his head, but not so much that it'll be too loose when I choke him out.

"Someone said Marcus came looking for information and was directed to you."

My lungs halt and a harsh thud slams in my chest. I ask him quietly, knowing the smirk on my face is dimming and finding it hard to swallow, "And who would that be?"

"Yours truly," he gives me the answer with his grin widening. "It was kind of a test," he tells me as I take in a single deep breath and grip the rope tightly with both hands, my thumbs running along the rough bundles that are fastened around both my hands. "And you failed, Sebastian." For the first time, his smile fades and he shrugs. "I'm sure there's a reason though," he says, feigning sympathy.

I nod once, making it look like I'm full of regret. And I am. I regret not killing this fucker sooner.

In one swift moment, my arms are up and around his head. He tries to turn and get out of my reach, but all that does is spin him around, so his back is to my chest as I get the rope right where I want it.

His feet come back first, trying to kick me as his hands reach up and try to grab the rope before it tightens. He gets the tip of two fingers in the loop, but I don't give a fuck. I'm squeezing so tight I can't breathe, I can't move. My muscles are on fire and my teeth grind together as I grunt out the pain. His large body slams into me, shoving me against the back wall. I grit my teeth as his boots squeak against the floor as he throws his head back into my shoulder.

He throws his body to the left, knocking us both into the tables and I almost lose my grip as I fall hard, smacking the side of my head against the edge of one chair as we tumble to the floor, but I hold on with everything I have, feeling the thin rope dig in deeper.

I watch his face closely, seeing how red his eyes are getting and how pale his face is.

His cheeks puff out as his strength wanes. Another kick, but this one's weaker. A few more seconds and his head lolls. I still can't breathe, and I pull back harder, feeling the rope nearly cut into his fingers, giving it more slack as the bones break. I hold on tight for another moment, and he doesn't react. He's limp and heavy, his dead eyes bloodshot and staring ahead at nothing.

When I finally release him, I have to slowly unwind the rope and bring the circulation back to my numb fingers. It's still dark as I pick up the chairs and tables, grabbing Eddie's corpse by the ankles to move him out of the way. There's no blood, no sign of a struggle. I check the wall we crashed into, feeling the burn and sting of my muscles. I'll bruise, but there's no dents or any sign of what happened. And that's what matters.

My shoulders burn as I drag his heavy ass to the back, kicking the swinging door open and pulling him through the kitchen to get to where the freezers are. He isn't the first and he won't be the last dead body to be stored here.

I shut the door hard, giving it the last of my anger and locking it with a loud click that resonates through every inch of me. My body is still on fire, my pulse hammering in my ears.

Shipments come on Mondays. I'll be long gone by then. I lock the freezer and look down at my hands. They're red and the skin is ripped from the rough rope digging into them. Swallowing thickly and breathing in deeply to calm the adrenaline still racing through me, I let a moment pass.

Sitting in the car, I'm still making sure I've thought through every bit of this.

Romano will send people to watch out for me to return, and he'll send people out looking for me, I know he will. He'll never find us though and I'm never coming back. I already know that.

Marcus will let me go, so long as everything happens the way it's supposed to tomorrow.

Carter though. I can't stop thinking about leaving him behind. Ever since we got in the car, I haven't let go of Chloe Rose's hand. She gives me the strength I've never had, but nothing can help me with this. With saying goodbye to him.

The keys jingle as I turn off the ignition after pulling up in front of Carter's house.

"Stay in the car," I tell her, turning off the headlights and passing the keys to her hand. Her fingers against mine still ignite something primitive and deep inside of me.

It stirs a warmth in my heart I never thought existed.

Her baby blue eyes plead with me not to stop, to just keep going and never look back. I lean forward, spearing my fingers in her hair and resting my forehead against hers. "I won't be long, I promise," I whisper against her lips.

She's quick to take a kiss, pressing her lips against mine and then pulling away to nuzzle the tip of her nose against mine.

"Kiss me first," she demands softly, with her eyes closed and her hands on my thigh. Her fingers lay across my jeans and when she tries to scoot closer to me, the sound of her nails against the denim is all I can hear along with my heart beating faster.

It beats fast and steady for her.

"I can tell that you love me when you kiss me," she whispers, her eyes looking deep into mine as the moonlight caresses her face. "Part of me can. Even if my mind can't keep up," she adds.

"Your mind can't keep up?" I ask her with a hint of a smile on my lip as I cup her chin. My gaze leaves her as I see a shadow on the sidewalk. Carter's outside and waiting for me.

Chloe shrugs, although it's a sad movement. "There's just something about the way you kiss me," she tells me.

"I love you, Chloe Rose," I tell her and as she parts her lips to tell me the same, I press my own against hers, slipping my tongue through the seam she gives me. She deepens the kiss, but for only a moment. My heart races and my blood heats.

She was always meant to be mine.

The second our lips part, both of us breathing heavier, she whispers, "I love you too."

I know she does, and with the parting thought, I open my door and close it as quietly as I can, so I can go to Carter.

My best friend. Only friend. And the only family I ever had.

"I was wondering if you'd come tonight," Carter says while I'm still a few feet away.

"Is that right?" I ask him as I walk up. Out here is more in the sticks than Dixon Street. All I can hear are grasshoppers and some kids playing ball in the street a block down.

Carter only nods in response and I can't fucking stand what I'm about to do.

"I have something to ask you," I start out and then backtrack. "How's it going? You guys doing all right?"

Carter gives me a weak smile and a half-assed laugh before kicking the ground. "Get on with it, man." His eyes reflect the way I feel. Like he already knows it's coming.

"Maybe we should settle the other thing first," I tell him, more willing to put an end to that shit than I am to say my final goodbye to him.

"Is it done?" Carter asks me the second I hesitate to speak. Standing outside of his house on the cracked sidewalk, he shoves both of his hands in his leather jacket pockets. He looks anxious as his eyes dart between the car and me. "I've got this feeling," he starts to tell me and then swallows visibly, before shaking his head.

I grip both of his shoulders and look him in the eyes. "It's done," I tell him with a strength that's undeniable. "Marcus left the cash yesterday."

"Cash?"

"I didn't know either. I thought it was, do what he said or die. I didn't expect the money."

Peeking over my shoulder, I take a look back at Chloe, my sweet innocent girl who will never know any of this shit. I'll protect her from it and from the man I was before her until my last breath. With the stack of cash in my pocket, I reach for it as I watch Chloe stare straight ahead at the dead-end street we'll never drive down again.

"Here it is," I say and hand it over to Carter, opening up his jacket and shoving it in before he can tell me he doesn't want it.

I'm the one who was told to kill them, all the names on the photocopy of the list that Marcus gave me. Marcus told me in the alley behind the butcher shop that he wanted information.

He gave me a list, and I was to get information for him and not say shit to Romano. I wasn't supposed to ask questions. There are whispers of Marcus, but no one ever sees him. He stays in shadows and they say if you ever see him, you're dead.

I was scared shitless that he chose me, and I was ready to do whatever he said to stay off his radar.

But her name was there.

It was right fucking there at the bottom of the list. I had to tell him whatever he wanted with this list, it couldn't be her. I had to beg for her life. He wanted them all dead. Every one of them.

Not her was all I could tell him.

However, he got a hold of Chloe's list, for whatever reason, she hadn't erased her name yet. The photocopy had her name there, written clearly at the bottom. And he'd added the last names in his own handwriting. At the time, I thought it was odd that two people had each written half of the names, but I never guessed it was her that wrote the list, I would never have known.

She'd made a list of who she blamed, or hated, I don't know which is more true. But Marcus decided it would be a hit list and now was the time for all of them to die.

I've never known fear like I did when I told Marcus it couldn't be her. I told him she couldn't die. Anyone but her.

He said he would spare her, but that he didn't want information anymore. He wanted them all dead in the span of three weeks and he didn't care how.

I bartered for her life, and then I killed them all. Each and every one. I set their deaths in motion. I paid off a thug with a pack of heroin to take care of Amber. Tamra was a bullet in her head. I can still hear the ringing in my ears. I'm a murderer.

But I did it to spare Chlo. I had to do it. I'd do it again if kept her safe. I don't care what kind of man that makes me, so long as she's still breathing.

Tomorrow is day twenty, leaving a single day to spare of his morbid deadline.

"Andrea picks up her package tomorrow. Can you just make sure she gets it?" I ask Carter. Andrea gets an eightball of coke on the regular. I knew that's how she needed to go when she came to the shop two weeks ago, but Marcus wanted them done in order. So, she had to wait until tomorrow.

Now I wonder if he requested that on purpose. If somehow, he knew it'd freak Chlo out and that's why he texted her the way he did.

He's a sick fuck, but I lived up to my end of the bargain.

"She's done, and it's done," I tell him. It's laced with so much shit, it'll be quick and easy. Marcus won't come looking for us. It'll all be over with.

We'll run away, and this nightmare will be over.

Dave was an accident, Carter's accident. He didn't know he was on the list, but Dave had it coming to him regardless, for what he did to Carter and his family. I could never blame Carter for what he did. It's his story to tell, even if it did fuck him up more than it should have. The fucker was going to die anyway. I told him that.

Carter's not a killer; he's not meant for this life.

"The money's yours. I can at least give you that," I tell him, knowing that money won't go far with the debt they have. But it's better than nothing.

"Take it back," Carter tells me angrily. "I don't want it."

253

"Maybe not, but you need it," I tell him, putting my hands up to refuse the money and then looking back to make sure Chloe can't see.

She can never know.

"I know you're leaving." Carter's voice breaks. I don't know how he knew. Word spreads fast, but if that's going around, Romano is going to hear it before long and that means I need to get the fuck out of here as fast as I can. I don't need him looking for me, or worse, finding the body I left in his shop before the weekly deliveries on Monday.

"Who told you?" I ask him, my pulse beating harder in my temples. My jaw stiffens with the fear of a fight coming.

"No one," he answers, "but I know when goodbyes are coming."

Time passes slowly, and I feel myself breaking down. My first reaction is to go to Chloe Rose. I forget it all with her. I forget who I am and all the pain that comes with it. With her, I'm not alone.

"You need it. You can't run far without cash." He gives me a look of complete sincerity as he pushes it back into my hand. "It's not for me, and I don't want it." His voice is clear like he knew I'd give it to him.

"I have enough cash," I tell him. "Take it for your brothers then." My heart squeezes harder in my chest knowing how fucked they all are. It's two grand, and two grand more than he'll get selling dope on the street corner like he thinks he can do. I worked for Romano, but Carter doesn't. And it's not safe.

Carter gives me a weak smile and shakes his head. "We'll be all right. I'm heading up to the north side. I'll take care of us." I know that means he's dealing something. Although what and for who, I don't know.

His eyes are so serious. He seems so much older to me now.

"You can come with me," I tell him. "I don't want to leave you here. Come with us."

The weak smile is pulled into a smirk, one cloaked with sadness. Goodbyes are never easy, but they shouldn't hurt this much. "Don't stay here," I beg him. "I want more for you than this."

"I can't leave my brothers," he tells me and then licks his lips before handing the money back to me. "Take it." The bills brush against my knuckles and I'm reluctant to take it, but I do. "Find a better place than here." The money weighs heavy in my hand as he pulls his away. I won't take it. If anything, I'll leave it in the mailbox and pray one of them finds it.

"It's good you're skipping out," Carter tells me in a tone that lets me know something's up.

"What's going on?" I ask him, feeling my nerves ramp up.

"I heard Eddie say Romano wants to talk to you on Monday. I think they know you're involved and they're pissed they didn't know."

"Good thing I won't be around Monday." I start thinking about all the possible outcomes of that meeting and I don't like a single one of them. I could never rat Marcus out, he'd kill me. And even if I did, Romano would kill me for following someone else's orders. I have protection from no one and enemies everywhere.

"Did you tell her?" Carter changes the subject abruptly. "Does she know you killed them?"

I shake my head, wishing all of this was a nightmare I could wake from. All of it but Chloe. "I had to lie to her, but it's never felt like that," I tell him, confiding in my best friend one last time.

"Felt like what?" he asks me.

"Felt like I was hurting her by lying to her. I've never wanted so much from someone and to give her so much in return."

He smiles a genuine but sad smile that reaches his dark eyes. "I knew you loved her," he says light-heartedly. Brushing his thumb against his nose, he peeks behind him. It's darker now than it was before, not a single star in the sky to cast light down on us.

"I think it is love," I tell him and kick the rubble on the broken concrete.

"It's all right to say it," he jokes, "I won't make fun of you."

"I only just got her. I can't lose her, Carter," I

confess to him. If it wasn't for her need to run away from here, I'd stay for him.

"Go ahead, I'll be all right," he tells me, and I want to believe him. "Hey, do you have that stuff though? Before you go?"

It takes me a minute to realize he's talking about the sweets. I have the last vial in my pocket and I know Chlo is never going to want to take it again, so I hand it over to him.

He's quick to slip the vial into his pocket. "Thanks, man. It's been rough sleeping."

Giving him a nod of understanding, I wonder if I should tell him that Chlo thinks some of her paranoia is from the drug, but I think she's wrong. She was right the entire time. Call it fear and intuition maybe.

"I hope it helps you sleep," I tell him and then glance back at the car.

"Get out of here, man. Get out while you still can," Carter tells me and it fucking hurts that I'm leaving him, but I have to. I have to get the hell out of here and take Chloe far away.

I have to reach out and hug him, pulling him hard into my chest. And he's quick to give me a hard pat on the back, followed by a grip I'll never forget.

There's no way I'd have made it out alive without him. I know that much.

Before the tears can show, I pull away from him, the only family I've ever had. "She can't stay here," I tell him as if I'm begging him to understand, but he already knows.

She's never belonged here.

"Come with us," I plead with him one last time even though I already know his answer.

"I have to stay." His voice is calm this time like he's resigned to his fate.

EPILOGUE

Two weeks later
Chloe

THE COOL WIND flows through my fingers as I rest my hand against the window. We've been off the highway for a little while now, still venturing into the unknown.

It's odd how the unfamiliar can offer so much comfort. How easy it is to leave everything behind and start a new life.

Countless times I've felt the fear of what could be waiting for us if we ever went back. And almost as if Bastian can read my mind, he asks me every time we stop somewhere new, "How about this place?"

"I can be a butcher anywhere. Or anything. We

can be anything," he keeps telling me. "Just don't leave me." He says that a lot. As if I'd ever want to. One day, I think he'll know in every way that I'll never do that.

In every beat of my heart, I know I was supposed to run away with him. And he was supposed to run away with me.

We should have left when we were only children. We shouldn't have stayed in that place as long as we did. When the lights around you flicker and dim, it's a sign to run. To run far away and toward light and hope. It's an innate feeling I knew deep in my gut, but I swallowed it down and nearly let the darkness choke out what little life I had left in me.

It's only taken days of being away with Bastian at my side, holding my hand as we drive farther and farther away to know that's true.

I can smell the salty ocean air as the sun kisses my skin through the window. We're close to the ocean.

A line springs to mind and I jot it down in my notebook. It's half-full already, with ideas for a book so close to what I've been through. Some changes here and there because it's hard to write about the truth. It's hard to imagine what people would think of me if I told them my story. It's even harder for me to write it all down and to be okay with everything that happened. Because of what happened in my life, the things that were done to me and the things I did... well, it will never be okay, but maybe it would make a memorable tale.

"Do you want to stop here?" Bastian asks, pointing to the left at a sign for a burger place.

My shoulders lift easily in a contented shrug. With my cheek resting against the headrest, I ask him for the tenth time since we left, "Where do you think we're going?" I need answers to what we'll become. I know I love him and I only want to be with him, but the stirring in my stomach that this is too good to be true hasn't let up.

Bastian's large hand wraps around mine as he pulls my knuckles to his lips to kiss them one by one. The car idles at the stop sign and he looks me deep in my eyes.

"We're going where we're supposed to go. Together." His words are a balm to my broken soul. It's the only word that matters. It's the only word that's ever mattered. *Together*.

With tears pricking my eyes, the tears I wish would go away, even if they are from a happiness I never thought I'd feel, I whisper, "I love you."

He braces his hands on either side of my head, stealing a ravenous kiss from me, taking my pain away like he did so many years ago. But the pain now is minuscule and it's because of him. He's taken it all away. And I'll spend my life making sure I do the same for him.

With a bruising kiss, I can hardly breathe until he pulls away from me, letting the tip of his nose brush against mine. His eyes are still closed, his hands still tangled in my hair as he tells me, "I've always loved you. And I'll never stop loving you. I'll always choose you."

* * *

Sebastian
Years later

ABOUT TWO WEEKS after we got in the car and sped away as fast as we could, I got a call from Carter's brother, Daniel. I didn't let her see as I broke down against the bathroom door of the motel we'd stayed in for the night. We'd move from one place to the next, constantly on the go until we found a spot on the West Coast, far away from Crescent Hills. A local bed and breakfast was looking to hire a butcher for their farm and also in need of a bookkeeper for the inn. Fate gave us our opportunity to stay, to find a new home, and we did. We grabbed it with both hands and didn't let go.

That night in the motel though, it almost didn't happen. The first few days we were on the road, everything changed with a single phone call. I almost got into the car and drove back to that hellhole when Daniel told me what happened. I would never have brought Chloe, but she wouldn't have let me leave her behind either.

The Talvery crew almost beat him to death the night we left. Carter nearly died for selling on the wrong turf. Daniel told me not to come back, that my name had been marked now, and I knew what that meant. If I went back, I was dead.

When I talked to Carter, I knew I'd made a mistake letting him stay. He had no one anymore, and everyone to provide for.

If I could go back, I would.

I'd never leave him behind.

It took over a decade before I dared show my face in that city again. Years of the phone calls coming less and less often. Years of building a life with the girl I always loved, while the memories of my past faded to bad dreams.

Life is a compromise. I left behind a friend, destined to stay, and be held captive to a city that had no mercy.

It would force him to become a brutal man I didn't recognize.

The Carter I abandoned in Crescent Hills, died that night I ran, and I'll never forgive myself for it.

The End.

* * *

Carter's story, Merciless, is available now!
Keep reading for a sneak peek …

CLICK here to sign up to my mailing list, where you'll get *exclusive* giveaways, free books and new release alerts!

* * *

FOLLOW me on BookBub to be the first to know about my sales!

TEXT ALERTS: Text WILLOW to 797979

AND IF YOU'RE on Facebook, join my reader group, Willow Winters' Wildflowers for special updates and lots of fun!

KEEP READING at the very end for a preview of my *USA Today* Bestseller, Something to Remember. Or you can start reading today for FREE!

Sinful Obsessions Series:

It's Our Secret

Little Liar

Possessive

Merciless

Standalone Novels:

Broken

Forget Me Not

Sins and Secrets Duets:

Imperfect (Imperfect Duet book 1)

Unforgiven (Imperfect Duet book 2)

Damaged (Damaged Duet book 1)

Scarred (Damaged Duet book 2)

Happy reading and best wishes,
W Winters xx

SNEAK PEEK OF POSSESSIVE

From *USA Today* bestselling author W Winters comes an emotionally gripping, standalone, contemporary romance.

It was never love with Daniel and I never thought it would be.

It was only lust from a distance.

Unrequited love maybe.

He's a man I could never have, for so many reasons.

That didn't stop my heart from beating wildly when his eyes pierced through me.

It only slowed back down when he'd look away, making me feel so damn unworthy and reminding me that he would never be mine.

Years have passed and one look at him brings it all back.

But time changes everything.

There's a heat in his eyes I recognize from so long ago, a tension between us I thought was one-sided.

"Tell me you want it." His rough voice cuts through the night and I can't resist.

That's where my story really begins.

Possessive is an emotional, gripping story. Filled with heartache, guilt and longing! Possessive will take you on a journey of obsession and jealousy...it's emotional, raw and captivating. - **Beyond The Covers Blog**

PREFACE

Addison

*I*t's easy to smile around Tyler.

It's how he got me. We were in tenth-grade calculus, and he made some stupid joke about angles. I don't even remember what it was. Something about never discussing infinity with a mathematician because you'll never hear the end of it. He's a cute dork with his jokes. He knows some dirty ones too.

A year later and he still makes me smile. Even when we're fighting. He says he just wants to see me smile. How could I leave when I believe him with everything in me?

My friend's grandmother told me once to fall in love with someone who loves you just a little more.

Even as my shoulders shake with a small laugh and he

leans forward nipping my neck, I know that I'll never really love Tyler the way he loves me.

And it makes me ashamed. Truly.

I'm still laughing when the bedroom door creaks open. Tyler plants a small kiss on my shoulder. It's not an open-mouth kiss, but still, it leaves a trace on my skin and sends a warmth through my body. It's only momentary though.

The cool air passes between the two of us, as Tyler leans back and smiles broadly at his brother.

I may be seated on my boyfriend's lap, but the way Daniel looks at me makes me feel alone. His eyes pierce through me. With a sharpness that makes me afraid to move. Afraid to breathe even.

I don't know why he does this to me.

He makes me hot and cold at the same time. It's like I've disappointed him simply by being here. As if he doesn't like me. Yet, there's something else.

Something that's forbidden.

It creeps up on me whenever I hear Daniel's rough voice; whenever I catch him watching Tyler and me. It's like I've been caught cheating, which makes no sense at all. I don't belong to Daniel, no matter how much that idea haunts my dreams.

He's almost twenty and I'm only sixteen. And more importantly, he's Tyler's brother.

It's all in my head. I tell myself over and over again that the electricity between us is something I've made up. That my body doesn't burn for Daniel. That my soul doesn't ache *for him to rip me away and punish me for daring to let his brother touch me.*

It's only when Tyler says something to him, that Daniel turns to look at him, tossing something down beside us.

Tyler's oblivious to everything happening. And suddenly, I can breathe again.

MY EYELIDS FLUTTER OPEN, my body hot under the stifling blankets. I don't react to the memory in my dreams anymore. Not at first. It sinks in slowly. The recognition of what that day would lead to getting heavier in my heart with each second that passes. Like a wave crashing on the shore, but it's taking its time. Threatening as it approaches.

It was years ago, but the memory stays.

The feeling of betrayal, for fantasizing about Tyler's older brother.

The heartache from knowing what happened only three weeks after that night.

The desire and desperation to go back to that point and beg Tyler to never come looking for me.

All of those needs stir into a deadly concoction in the pit of my stomach. It's been years since I've been tormented by the memories of Tyler and what we had. And by the memories of Daniel and what never was.

Years have passed.

But it all comes back now that Daniel's back.

CHAPTER 1

Addison
The night before

I LOVE THIS BAR. Iron Heart Brewery. It's nestled in the center of the city and located at the corner of this street. The town itself has history. Hints of the old cobblestone streets peek through the torn asphalt and all the signs here are worn and faded, decorated with weathered paint. I can't help but to be drawn here.

And with the varied memorabilia lining the walls, from signed knickknacks to old glass bottles of liquor, this place is flooded with a welcoming warmth. It's a quiet bar with all local and draft beers a few blocks away from the chaos of campus. So it's just right for me.

"Make up your mind?"

My body jolts at the sudden question. It only gets me a rough laugh from the tall man on my left, the bartender who spooked me. A grey shirt with the brewery logo on it fits the man well, forming to his muscular shoulders. With a bit of stubble and a charming smirk, he's not bad looking. And at that thought, my cheeks heat with a blush.

I could see us making out behind the bar; I can even hear the bottles clinking as we crash against the wall in a moment of passion. But that's where it would end for me. No hot and dirty sex on the hard floor. No taking him back to my barely furnished apartment.

I roll my eyes at the thought and blow a strand of hair away from my face as I meet his gaze.

I'm sure he flirts with everyone. But it doesn't make it any less fun for the moment.

"Whatever your favorite is," I tell him sheepishly. "I'm not picky." I have to press my lips together and hold back my smile when he widens his and nods.

"You new to town?" he asks me.

I shrug and have to slide the strap to my tank top back up onto my shoulder. Before I can answer, the door to the brewery and bar swings open, bringing in the sounds of the nightlife with it. It closes after two more customers leave. Looking over my shoulder through the large glass door at the front, I can see them heading out. The woman is leaning heavily against a strong man who's obviously her significant other.

Giving the bartender my attention again, I'm very much aware that there are only six of us here now. Two older men at the high top bar, talking in hushed voices and occasionally laughing so loud that I have to take a peek at them.

And one other couple who are seated at a table in the corner of the bar. The couple who just left had been sitting with them. All four are older than I am. I'd guess married with children and having a night out on the town.

And then there's the bartender and me.

"I'm not really from here, no."

"Just passing through?" he asks me as he walks toward the bar. I'm a table away, but he keeps his eyes on me as he reaches for a glass and hits the tap to fill it with something dark and decadent.

"I'm thinking about going to the university actually. To study business. I came to check it out." I don't tell him that I'm putting down some temporary roots regardless of whether or not I like the school here. Every year or so I move somewhere new … searching for what could feel like home.

His eyebrow raises and he looks me up and down, making me feel naked. "Your ID isn't fake, right?" he asks and then tilts the tall glass in his hand to let the foam slide down the side.

"It isn't fake, I swear," I say with a smile and hold up my hands in defense. "I chose to travel instead of going to college. I've got a little business, but I thought finally learning more about the technicalities of it all would be a step in the right direction." I pause, thinking about how a degree feels more like a distraction than anything else. It's a reason to settle down and stop moving from place to place. It could be the change I need. Something needs to change.

His expression turns curious and I can practically hear all the questions on his lips. *Where did you go? What did you do? Why did you leave your home so young and naïve?* I've heard them all before and I have a prepared list of answers in my head for such questions.

But they're all lies. Pretty little lies.

He cleans off the glass before walking back over and pulling out the seat across from me.

Just as the legs of the chair scrape across the floor, the door behind me opens again, interrupting our conversation and the soft strums of the acoustic guitar playing in the background.

The motion brings a cold breeze with it that sends goosebumps down my shoulder and spine. A chill I can't ignore.

The bartender's ass doesn't even touch the chair. Whoever it is has his full attention.

As I lean down to reach for the cardigan laying on

top of my purse, he puts up a finger and mouths, "One second."

The smile on my face is for him, but it falters when I hear the voice behind me.

Everything goes quiet as the door shuts and I listen to them talking. My body tenses and my breath leaves me. Frozen in place, I can't even slip on the cardigan as my blood runs cold.

My heart skips one beat and then another as a rough laugh rises above the background noise of the small bar.

"Yeah, I'll take an ale, something local," I hear Daniel say before he slips into view. I know it's him. That voice haunted me for years. His strides are confident and strong, just like I remember them. And as he passes me to take a seat by the bar, I can't take my eyes off of him.

He's taller and he looks older, but the slight resemblance to Tyler is still there. As my heart learns its rhythm again, I notice his sharp cheekbones and my gaze drifts to his hard jaw, covered with a five o'clock shadow. I'd always thought of him as tall and handsome, albeit in a dark and brooding way. And that's still true.

He could fool you with his charm, but there's a darkness that never leaves his eyes.

His fingers spear through his hair as he checks out the beer options written in chalk on the board behind the bar. His hair's longer on top than it is on the sides, and I can't help but to imagine what it would feel like to grab on to it. It's a fantasy I've always had.

The timbre in his voice makes my body shudder.

And then heat.

I watch his throat as he talks, I notice the little movements as he pulls out a chair in the corner of the bar across from me. If only he would look my way, he'd see me.

Breathe. Just breathe.

My tongue darts out to lick my lips and I try to avert my eyes, but I can't.

I can't do a damn thing but wait for him to notice me.

I almost whisper the command, *look at me.* I think it so loud I'm sure it can be heard by every soul in this bar.

And finally, as if hearing the silent plea, he looks my way. His knuckles rap the table as he waits for his beer, but they stop mid-motion when his gaze reaches mine.

There's a heat, a spark of recognition. So intense and so raw that my body lights, every nerve ending alive with awareness.

And then it vanishes. Replaced with a bitter chill as he turns away. Casually. As if there was nothing there. As if he doesn't even recognize me.

I used to think it was all in my mind back then. Five

years ago when we'd share a glance and that same feeling would ignite within me.

But this just happened. I know it did.

And I know he knows who I am.

With anger beginning to rise, my lips part to say his name, but it's caught in my throat. It smothers the sadness that's rising just as quickly. Slowly my fingers curl, forming a fist until my nails dig into my skin.

I don't stop staring at him, willing him to look at me and at least give me the courtesy of acknowledging me.

I know he can feel my eyes on him. He's stopped rapping his knuckles on the table and the smile on his face has faded.

Maybe the crushing feeling in my chest is shared by both of us.

Maybe I'm only a reminder to him. A reminder he ran away from too.

I don't know what I expected. I've dreamed of running into Daniel so many nights. Brushing shoulders on the way into a coffee shop. Meeting each other again through new friends. Every time I wound up back home, if you can even call it that, I always checked out every person passing me by, secretly wishing one would be him. Just so I'd have a reason to say his name.

Winding up at the same bar on a lonely Tuesday night hours away from the town we grew up in … that was one of those daydreams too. But it didn't go like this in my head.

"Daniel." I say his name before I can stop myself. It comes out like a croak and he reluctantly turns his head as the bartender sets down the beer on the wooden table.

I swear it's so quiet, I can hear the foam fizzing as it settles in the glass.

His lips part just slightly, as if he's about to speak. And then he visibly inhales. It's a sharp breath and matches the gaze he gives me. First it's one of confusion, then anger … and then nothing.

I have to remind my lungs to do their job as I clear my throat to correct myself, but both efforts are in vain.

He looks past me as if it wasn't me who was trying to get his attention.

"Jake," he speaks up, licking his lips and stretching his back. "I actually can't stay," he bellows from his spot to where the bartender, apparently named Jake, is chucking ice into a large glass. The music seems to get louder as the crushing weight of being so obviously dismissed and rejected settles in me.

I'm struck by how cold he is as he gets up. I can't stand to look at him as he readies to leave, but his name leaves me again. This time with bite.

His back stiffens as he shrugs his thin jacket around his shoulders and slowly turns to look at me.

I can feel his eyes on me, commanding me to look back at him and I do. I dare to look him in the eyes and say, "It's good to see you." It's surprising how even the words come out. How I can appear to be so calm when inside I'm burning with both anger and ... something else I don't care to admit. What a lie those words are.

I hate how he gets to me. How I never had a choice.

With a hint of a nod, Daniel barely acknowledges me. His smile is tight, practically nonexistent, and then he's gone.

Possessive is Available Now!

SNEAK PEEK OF FORGET ME NOT

I fell in love with a boy a long time ago.

I was only a small girl. Scared and frightened, I was taken from my home and held against my will. His father hurt me, but he protected me and kept me safe as best he could.

Until I left him.

I ran the first chance I got and even though I knew he wasn't behind me, I didn't stop. The branches lashed out at me, punishing me for leaving him in the hands of a monster.

I've never felt such guilt in my life.

Although I survived, the boy was never found. I prayed for him to be safe. I dreamed he'd be alright and come back to me. Even as a young girl I knew I loved him, but I betrayed him.

Twenty years later, all my wishes came true.

But the boy came back a man. With a grip strong enough to keep me close and a look in his eyes that warned me to never dare leave him again. I was his to keep after all.

Twenty years after leaving one hell, I entered another. Our tale was only just getting started.

It's dark and twisted.

But that doesn't make it any less of what it is.

A love story. Our love story.

PROLOGUE

Robin

I can wait here longer than he can stand to stay away. I know that much.

A small grin pulls at my lips as I pick at the thread on the comforter. Always picking and waiting. There's nothing else to do in this room.

My head lifts at the thought, drawing my eyes to the blinking red light. And he's always watching. The sight of the camera makes my stomach churn, but only for a moment.

The sound of heavy boot steps walking down the stairs outside the closed door makes my heart race. I stare at the doorknob, willing it to turn and bring him to me.

I've waited too long for him.

The sound of the door opening is foreboding. If anyone other than me was waiting for him, I'd assume they'd have terror in their hearts. But I know him. I understand it all. The pain, the guilt. I know firsthand what it's like when the monster is gone and you only have your own thoughts to fight. Your memories and regrets. It's all-consuming.

And there's no one who can understand you. No one you trust, whose words you can believe are genuine and not just disguised pity.

But he knows me, and I know him. Far too well; our pain is shared.

His broad shoulders fill the doorway and his dark eyes meet mine instantly. He barely touches the door and it closes behind him with a loud click that's only a hair softer than my wildly beating heart.

It's hard to swallow, but I do. And I ignore the heat, the quickened breath. I push it all down as he walks toward me, closing the space with one heavy step at a time.

He stops in front of me, but doesn't hesitate to cup my chin in his large hand and I lean into his comforting touch. I know to keep my own hands down though and I grip the comforter instead of him.

It's a violent pain that rips through me, knowing how scarred he is. So much so, that I have to hold back everything. I'm afraid of my words, my touch. He's so close to being broken beyond repair and I only want to save him, but I don't know how.

We're both damaged, but the tortured soul in front of me makes me feel everything. He makes me want to live and heal his tormented soul. But how can I, when I'm the one who broke him by running away?

"My little bird," he whispers and it reminds me of when we were children. When we were trapped together.

He's not the boy who protected me.

He's not the boy whose eyes were filled with a darkness barely tempered with guilt.

He's not the boy I betrayed the moment I had a chance.

He's a man who's taking what he wants.

AND THAT'S ME.

Robin

One week before

"Doctor Everly?" a soft voice calls out, breaking me from my distant thoughts as another early spring chill whips through my thin jacket and sends goosebumps down my body. I slowly turn my head to Karen. Her cheeks are a little too pink from a combination of the harsh wind and a heavy-handed application of blush, and the tip of her nose is a bright red.

I grip my thin jacket closer, huddling in it as if it can protect me from the brutal weather. It's too damn cold for spring, but I suppose I'd rather be cold and uncomfortable out here. Today especially.

I give Karen a tight smile, although I don't know why. It's not polite to smile out here, or is it? "How are you doing?" I ask her as she walks closer to me.

She nods her head, taking in a breath and looking past me at the pile of freshly upturned dirt. "It hurts still. It's just so sad." Karen's only twenty-three, fresh out of college and new to this. I'm new to it too. Marie was the first patient I've had who killed herself.

Sad isn't the right word for it. Devastating doesn't even begin to describe what it feels like when a young girl in your care decides her life is no longer worth living.

I clear my throat and turn on the grass to face her. The thin heels of my shoes sink into the soft ground, and I have to balance myself carefully just to stand upright.

"It is," I tell Karen, not sure what else to say.

"How do you handle…" her voice drifts off.

I don't know how to answer her. My lips part and I shake my head, but no words come out.

"I'm so sorry, Robin," she says and Karen's voice is strong and genuine. She knows how much Marie meant to me. But it wasn't enough.

I try to give her an appreciative smile, but I can't. Instead, I clear my tight throat and nod once, looking back to where Marie's buried.

"Are you okay?" she asks me cautiously, resting a

hand on my arm, trying to comfort me. And I do what I shouldn't. *I lie.*

"I'm okay," I tell her softly, reaching up to squeeze her hand.

As I tuck a loose strand of hair behind my ear, a gust of wind flies by us and a bolt of lightning splits the sky into pieces, followed a few seconds later with the hard crack of thunder.

Karen looks up, and in an instant the light gray clouds darken and cue the storm to set in. It's only the two of us left here and it looks like the weather won't have us here any longer, leaving Marie all alone. I think deep inside that's how she wanted it all along. She didn't want a shrink to give her advice.

Who was I to help her? The guilt washes through me and the back of my eyes prick with unshed tears as I take in a shuddering breath, shoving my hands in my pockets and turning back to her grave.

As much as I'd like to believe I'll let her rest now, I know I'll be back. It's selfish of me. She just wanted to be left alone. She needed that so her past could fade into the background. I know that now; I wish I knew it then.

"She's in a better place," Karen whispers and my gaze whips up to hers. She doesn't have the decency to look me in the eyes and I have to wonder if she just said the words because she thinks they're appropriate.

Like it's something meant to be said when talking of the dead, or maybe she really believes it.

Karen turns to walk toward her car as the sprinkling of rain starts to fall onto us. She looks back over her shoulder, waiting for me and I relent, joining her.

I'm sorry, Marie.

As the cold drops of rain turn to sheets and my hair dampens, my pace picks up. It doesn't take long until we're both jogging through the grass and then onto the pavement of the parking lot, our heels clicking and clacking on the pavement with the sound of the rain.

I barely hear her say goodbye and manage a wave behind me as I open my car door and sink into the driver seat.

I just wanted to help Marie. I could see so much of myself in her. We were almost the same age. She had the same look in her eyes. The same helplessness and lack of self-worth. I wanted to save her like my psychiatrist saved me.

But how could I? I'm not over my past. I should have known better. I should have referred her to someone more capable. Someone who had less emotional investment. I pushed too hard. *It's my fault.*

The pattering of rain on the car roof is eerily rhythmic as I dig through my purse, shivering and shoving the wet hair out of my face. The keys jingle as I shove them into the ignition, turning on the car and filling the cabin with the sounds of the radio.

I'm not sure what song's on but I don't care because I'm quick to turn the radio off. To get back to the silence and the peace of the rainfall. I slump in my seat, staring at the temperature gauge. When I look up, I see Karen drive away in the rearview mirror. Watching her car drive out of sight, my eyes travel to my reflection.

I scoff at myself and wipe under my eyes. I look dreadful. My dirty blonde hair's damp and disheveled, my makeup's running. I lift the console and grab a few tissues to clean myself up before sluggishly removing my soaked jacket and tossing it in the backseat. The heater finally kicks on, and I still can't bring myself to leave.

I look back into the mirror and see that I'm somewhat pulled together, but I can't hide the bags under my eyes. I can't force a false sense of contentment onto my face.

I close my eyes and take in another deep breath, filling my lungs and letting it out slowly. I need sleep. I need to eat. It's been almost a week since I found out about Marie. A week of her no longer being here to call and check in on. Tears stream freely down my cheeks. I tried so hard not to cry; I learned a long time ago that crying doesn't help, but being forced to leave her is making me helpless to my emotions.

That first night I almost cried, but instead I resorted to sleeping pills. A wave of nausea churns in my stomach at the thought of what I did. It was so easy to just take one after the other. Each one telling me it'd be over soon. After downing half the bottle, I knew what I was doing. But the entire bottle was too much and it all came back up before I could finish it. Thank God for that. I'm not well, and I'm sure as hell not in a position to help others.

My hand rests against my forehead as I try to calm down, as I try to rid myself of the vision of Marie in my office, but other memories of my past persist there, waiting for this weakness.

I can't linger any longer. Putting the car into reverse, I back out of my spot, turning and seeing Marie's plot in the distance as I back up.

Grief is a process, but guilt is something entirely different. It's becoming harder and harder to separate the two, and I know why.

She reminds me of *him*.

Of a boy, I knew long ago. The turn signal seems louder than ever as I wait at the exit to turn onto the highway. *Click, click, click.*

Each is a second of time that I'm here and they're not. *Click, click, click.*

The cabin warms as I drive away, merging onto the highway.

Maybe all this has nothing to do with Marie.

Maybe it's just the guilt that summons the vision of his light gray eyes from the depths of my memory.

Maybe it's because I'm to blame for both of their deaths.

Forget Me Not is Available Now!

ABOUT W WINTERS

Thank you so much for reading my romances. I'm just a stay at home mom and avid reader turned author and I couldn't be happier.
I hope you love my books as much as I do!

More by W Winters
www.willowwinterswrites.com/books/

Made in the USA
Middletown, DE
08 July 2023

34732668R00179